SPACE COMMAND

# JOURNEY INTO THE UNIVERSE

BOOK- 2

THE JOURNEY
CONTINUES

G.M. Leahy

Order this book online at www.trafford.com/08-1194
or email orders@trafford.com

Most Trafford titles are also available at major online book retailers.


Edited by Alice E. Pinero
Edited by Debra A. Leahy
Cover Illustration by J.F. Leahy


Note for Librarians: A cataloguing record for this book is available from Library and Archives Canada at www.collectionscanada.ca/amicus/index-e.html

ISBN: 978-1-4251-8690-6

*We at Trafford believe that it is the responsibility of us all, as both individuals and corporations, to make choices that are environmentally and socially sound. You, in turn, are supporting this responsible conduct each time you purchase a Trafford book, or make use of our publishing services. To find out how you are helping, please visit www.trafford.com/responsiblepublishing.html*

*Our mission is to efficiently provide the world's finest, most comprehensive book publishing service, enabling every author to experience success. To find out how to publish your book, your way, and have it available worldwide, visit us online at www.trafford.com/10510*

www.trafford.com

**North America & international**
toll-free: 1 888 232 4444 (USA & Canada)
phone: 250 383 6864 • fax: 250 383 6804 • email: info@trafford.com

**The United Kingdom & Europe**
phone: +44 (0)1865 487 395 • local rate: 0845 230 9601
facsimile: +44 (0)1865 481 507 • email: info.uk@trafford.com

10 9 8 7 6 5 4 3 2

# Contents

CHAPTER 1

# ROUGH RIDE

Captain Yates was in his quarters busy finishing up work on the ship's log. He finished his task and decided to take a short break before looking over a stack of status reports that were piled up on his desk. He reached down into the top draw of his desk and pulled out a compact disk by one of his favorite artist Enya and inserted it into his player. He set the music at a low volume and then poured himself a small glass of Jamison's.

Yates leaned back in his chair sipping on his drink and reflected on what he and his shipmates had gone through over the past few months. The crew had consisted mostly of greenhorns and had witnessed more in a short period of time than most people would have experienced in a lifetime. They had discovered new technology from exiled aliens on the planet Mars, traveled through a wormhole that had transported them to a distant part of the universe, nearly causing their demise. They revived an alien civilization and had done battle with them after they proved to be hostile. The crew fought an evil creature and destroyed it when they met a derelict ship in their travels through space. The men and women of CONSTELLATION formed an everlasting friendly relationship with the people of Flox and rescued them from a hostile take over from the Bedzals. The crew of CONSTELLATION had proved victorious with every obstacle that had faced them. With all the successes now a part of the ship's history, the captain just couldn't help thinking about his crew members who had lost their lives. As he pictured the faces of the departed, he trembled from the pain and the anguish that so often comes with the decisions of command.

The captain was almost in a trance when he was brought back to his senses by a knock on his cabin door. "Enter, it's open."

Commander Edwards walked in and started to ask a question, when he noticed the disturbed look on the captain's face.

"What's wrong Al, it looks like something is bothering you. What is it?" Edwards inquired.

"I don't know, maybe it's nothing. I can't help thinking about Stevens, Evans and the rest of the men who are no longer with us. I keep blaming myself for their deaths," the captain replied.

"Al, it's not your fault that we are here lost in God knows where. You didn't make the decision to come out here," Edwards responded.

Yates continued on, "No, you're wrong, it was my choice to leave the orbit around earth. If we would just have stayed put, hell, who knows, we just might be back on earth sitting back with our families instead we just may be spending the rest of our lives lost, trying to find our way back home."

"Captain, we all shared in the decision to set out and explore things. The burden is not entirely yours to bear. Don't do this to yourself. We were all excited to find out what was out here. We came across some incredible discoveries, but sadly enough there was a price to pay. Nothing comes cheap," Edwards added.

"Ralph, thank you, yes we did all agree that exploring would be better than just sitting above the earth going around in circles, but somehow I still feel responsible for our losses. Excuse me, you stopped by for a reason. What did you need?" Yates asked.

"I was on my way to meet Fisher at the mess hall and get some chow. I just stopped by to see if you would be interested in joining us," Edwards replied.

Captain Yates accepted his invitation and both men proceeded to the officer's mess. Upon arrival, the two officers got their chow and sat down at a table with Col. Fisher.

"Gentlemen, welcome. The grub here ain't too bad, sure beats the hell out of M.R.E.'s", Fisher said jokingly.

Yates replied, "No, it's not too bad. However, I'd give anything for some fresh lobster and a side of cole slaw."

Edwards joined in and said, "Not me, I'd love to have a nice juicy New York strip, medium rare, smothered in mushrooms and onions."

The conversation went on for a while about their favorite dishes and then gradually changed to the past events that had taken placed on the mission, then to what they would do when they got home. The three men were just about to get up from the table when the ship's P.A. system barked out, "Captain to the bridge, Captain Yates to the bridge."

Yates and Edwards excused themselves and headed to the bridge. As the two officers entered the ships command center they observed LCDR Wang, who was on watch, exiting the search center.

"What's going on?" Yates asked.

LCDR Wang replied, "Captain, Lieutenants Marsh and Williams have picked up some kind of abnormality on their screens. The irregularity is quite a distance off, but they feel it's worth investigating."

Yates, Edwards and Wang entered the search center to question Marsh and Williams.

Yates asked, "What do you have, boys?

LT Williams answered, "Sir, if you look at the screen right here." He pointed to a small blip. "This wrinkle may be what we are looking for. It just may be our ride home. It is a large distortion and it is a long way off. It seems to be coming from behind this solar system on the upper right corner of the screen."

Commander Edwards chimed in with, "Steve, is this a black hole or is it a worm hole? Let's make sure we know what we are headed for, or we could be in for one hell of a shock when we hit the pot hole."

Williams replied, "Sirs and mam, it looks like the real thing. As I said, we are quite a distance from it, but I think it's worth a gander."

Yates ordered Williams to give the coordinates to the helmsman, to plot a course, and to increase the speed of the ship. CONSTELLATION changed her course and proceeded at three-quarters speed to where the abnormality was.

Yates had Commander Edwards call all department heads to the bridge conference room for a short meeting, wanting to advise them of a possible return ticket to earth.

The officers arrived and the meeting started off with Yates making a statement, "O.K. folks it looks like we MAY have found a worm hole and we have changed course for it. It's some distance off, but this gives us time to prepare for it. We all know what happened the last time we went through one. Let's put our time to good use and prepare the ship for the rough ride. Instruct your people too batten down anything that is loose. When we get a little closer, have all non-essential electrical items turned off. We will need to conserve as much power as possible. With any luck we won't wind up in as bad of shape as we did the last time."

Colonel Fisher offered some help. "If anyone needs additional hands to prepare your areas for the ride, get a hold of me or Major Kinkaid and we will send some of our boys over to help out."

Yates and Edwards thanked the colonel for his offer. Yates advised that he wanted one of his flag officers in the search center at all times to oversee the mission in case any decisions had to be made at a moments notice. Both Edwards and Hall advised they would take the search center watch and devise a schedule between them to have it covered at all times. Yates opened the floor to questions, and there being none he dismissed the officers and headed back to the search center along with Commander Edwards and LCDR Hall.

As they entered the center they observed Marsh and Williams standing over the screen, scratching their heads looking dumbfounded.

Yates asked, "What's the problem?"

Marsh answered, "Captain, I don't know. One second the abnormality was there then it was gone, it came back and now it's gone. Wait, now it's back."

LCDR Hall went over and looked at the computer print out, he then started to scratch his head and said. "Yep, the boys are right this thing is there and then it's not. I'm just wondering if we are too far out for the equipment to keep a constant reading on it."

Yates responded. "That may be the case - we should know soon if that is the problem. As we close in on the target we should get stronger readings. Keep me posted. Also, I want a sharp crew on this. Between the four of you, I want two on and two off. It's up to you how you want to divide out the time. I'll be down in AIR OPS with Lewis. We may want to send out a scout ship."

Captain Yates made his way down to the Air Operations Office and met with LCDR Lewis. They were discussing sending out an F-56-A or an ASC-1 fitted out with a special signal enhancer on it to help boost the signal imagery for the Search Center. With a clearer signal it would be easier for the search Center staff to confirm that it was the worm hole they were looking for.

Yates and Lewis had finished their conversation and both agreed that a scout ship would be launched in the morning. They were having coffee sharing embellished war stories when they felt the ship start to shutter and then shake for a couple of seconds, then it stopped.

Yates, looking bewildered at Lewis questioned, "What the hell was that?"

Lewis, in an alarmed voice replied, "I'll be damned if I know, but it can't be fucking good!"

Yates phoned the bridge and was transferred to LCDR Hall, who was still in the Search Center. "Randy, what the hell was that shutter, did we hit something?"

Hall answered, "Captain, I don't know what it was. We didn't hit anything, the screens are all clear. Hold on a second sir, I have LCDR Malloy on the other line."

The captain held on and within three minutes LCDR Hall was back with him.

"Captain, I just spoke with Chet down in engineering, he advises that it wasn't anything with the engines. He did however notice there was a slight power drain during the episode, but things went back to normal as soon as it ended."

Yates advised him to remain at his station, he would be there momentarily. Both Captain Yates and LCDR Lewis were on their way up to the bridge when the ship started to shutter and shake for a second time - this time with more force. The ship was still feeling the effects from the unknown element as the lights dimmed for just a fraction of a second. Then all seemed normal again.

Yates and Lewis made their way to the bridge and went directly into the search Center. As they walked in the captain queried, "Randy, what the hell is going on? Are we being attacked or what?"

LCDR Hall replied, "Captain, it's the same as before, there ain't nothing out there. I don't know what the hell is causing this."

Just as the captain was about to ask another question the phone rang. Commander Edwards answered it, it was LCDR Malloy. The phone conversation lasted about five minutes then Edwards hung up. He looked over to the captain and said, "Al, that was Malloy in engineering, he advised that we had a deeper power drain this time during the episode. He and his staff have checked and doubled checked the entire system and they can't find anything internal that is causing the tremors. It has to be coming from someplace outside."

The Captain then ordered, "Reduce speed to one-quarter, I want a 360 degree maximum radar scan of the whole area. Doug, for the time being, scuttle the scouting mission. What ever is hitting the ship will probably tear a fighter apart if it got caught in it."

Before the captain's orders could be carried out, the ship was hit for a third time - the most intense so far. The crew had to grab a hold of anything stationary just to keep their balance. The captain then ordered the ship to general quarters. GONG, GONG, GONG the alarm sounded all through the ship.

"GENERAL QUARTERS, GENERAL QUARTERS, ALL HANDS MAN YOUR STATIONS. THIS IS NOT A DRILL," blared over the P.A. system.

The crew scrambled to man their stations and within moments all departments reported ready.

The captain and the X.O. were in their command chairs in the center upper tier of the bridge confirming the ship's ready status when LT Marsh came running out of the search center yelling.

"CAPTAIN, CAPTAIN, I know what it is. We are not under attack. The ship is being hit by a natural phenomenon."

"Lieutenant, are you sure? What kind of data do you have?" Yates questioned.

"Sir, I've been tracking the signals from the other side of the solar system. I have entered time and distance, our speed, the wave's speed, and everything checks out. We are not heading for a wormhole; we have gotten ourselves caught right in the middle of an escalating magnetic solar storm. The intensity is building at an alarming rate. We won't be able to outrun it."

"What do you mean we can't outrun it? What if we reverse course and head out at flank speed?" Yates asked.

LT Marsh stood there for a couple of moments then the captain grilled him for an answer. "Well mister, what do you mean, give me an answer. Speak to me."

"Sir, the waves are coming at faster intervals and at a higher intensity. Each time the ship is hit it has a negative effect on our power. It neutralizes our power from the depolarizing attributes of the magnetic surges of the storm. If we can't find a protective shield, such as a planet's atmosphere, the ship will be dead in space and most likely torn to pieces."

"Ralf, how far are we from the nearest planet system?" Yates asked.

"Captain, the closest one is dead ahead, in the same direction of the storm's origin. It will certainly be a challenge to see if we can make it to safety before the storm kills us off," Commander Edwards answered.

"Captain, I just went over LT Marsh's calculations, I think he is correct. We need to find a safe haven to land Connie on and weather the storm out there," LCDR Hall injected.

"O.K., we need to go head on into this thing and find a hideaway. Look's like we will be in for a rough ride. Randy, start scanning the planets in that system and try to find a friendly one fast. LT Marsh, good job son."

LCDR Hall proceeded scanning the solar system's planets as per the captain's orders. Out of the six planets scanned it seemed the only one that looked like it might have a friendly environment was the third one from the sun. Hall reported his findings to Yates.

The magnetic storm caused by the solar flares of the sun was growing stronger and the shock waves increased in frequency. Each time the CONSELLATION was hit she shook harder and the power drain on the ship's resources became more severe.

CONSTELLATION cleared the first two outer planets and it became harder to control the ship as she passed through each wave of the storm. The power drains were more severe and lasted for a longer period of time with each occurrence. Yates called down to the engineering department and conferred with LCDR Malloy on what measures could be taken to conserve power.

Malloy gave his recommendations to the captain. "Sir, I think we should take all nonessential systems off line immediately. I also think that all weapons systems should be taken down. This will save us about thirty percent drainage. With any luck, this might buy us some time and distance. I have Washington booting up all of the emergency generators, which should help stabilize the ship whenever we pass through the magnetic waves."

"Chet, I'll have Edwards go through the ship and shut down the systems. I'm concerned about getting nailed by one of those waves while we're in the process of landing the ship. Can we handle it?" the captain inquired.

"Captain, if we put into a low orbit and time our descent between the waves, we should be able to make it. Even in a low orbit we will get some shielding from the storm."

"Thanks Chet, I'll get the information entered into the navigational system. Keep me updated on any problems you encounter with our power."

Yates advised Commander Edwards to tour the ship and take all nonessential systems off line. Edwards left the bridge immediately to carry out the captain's orders. Data for the ship's orbit was entered into the navigational computers and CONSTELLATION, badly shaken from the magnetic storm arrived at the third planet and entered into a low orbit. As predicted, this orbit did provide some shielding from the storm however the intensity of each wave was eating away at the margin of safety gained.

The stormed proved to be too dangerous for a fighter to be launched to survey the planet's surface to find a suitable landing site for the ship. Yates ordered a probe be launched to gain the needed data. Soon the unmanned eyes for CONSTELLATION reported back to the ship's electronic brain that it had found a spot large and hard enough to support the ship's massive weight and the order was given to land Connie at that site.

CONSTELLATION started her downward approach just as one

of the magnetic waves hit the planet's atmosphere. The ship's power gave way and she started to plummet towards the planet's surface. Helm control was lost and the ship was fast approaching the point of no return for a safe landing. With the ship out of control, she was heating up fast as she cut through atmosphere. The ship was glowing red and the nose was well into white hot. CONSTELLATION was starting to burn up!

Yates got on the PA system and commanded, "Shut down all systems NOW! Engineering, transfer all power to helm control." His orders were carried out with lightening speed.

The surge of power that came from shutting down all other internal systems came just in the nick of time. Helm control was restored and Connie's nose started to lift up. The ship, now entirely white hot started to cool down to a soft red glow and then her true colors slowly returned to her outer hull as she leveled her descent.

LCDR Wang called up to the bridge, "Captain, power to life support needs to be returned now. The temperature is over 120 degrees in here - the plants are showing signs of stress. Without lowering the temperature we will start to loose them."

Yates checked with engineering on the power situation and LCDR Malloy advised that the danger, for the most part, was coming to an end. Power could be restored to each of the ship's systems on a priority basis. As Connie headed to her landing site, the ship's systems were tested one by one and if no problems were found they were put back on line. Due to the immense heat the ship suffered, problems anywhere from short circuits to completely melted components. These would need to be repaired when the ship was safely on the ground.

Connie reached her landing zone and touched down without any further incident. As when the ship touched down on Viron, Col. Fisher had his troops build an earthen fortress around

CONSTELLATION and security teams were put in place to guard CONSTELLATION from any unknown hostile force.

CHAPTER 2

# PARADISE OF BLOOD

Captain Yates, Col. Fisher and LCDR Hall met inside the hanger deck and proceeded to the outside of the ship and climbed onto the top of the earthen embankment just off the starboard bow of CONSTELLATION. After reaching the crest of the mound the three officers turned to observe the defenses that were being put into place to protect Connie in case of trouble. The tanks were paired off with Bradley Fighting Vehicles that were strategically parked along the fortifications inside perimeter. Machine guns were placed every one hundred yards on the top of the earth mounds with sharpshooters stationed in between the 50 calibers. Several F-56-A's and ASC-1's were also stationed to aft of Connie for a quick take off if so needed to defend the fortress.

The officers studied the defenses for a while and concluded that all the necessary precautions were being put into place. As they were turning around to head back to the ship, they stopped to gander at the surrounding scenery outside of the fortress. The foliage consisted of lavish, tall, bushy trees and shrubs. The plants and trees were lush with buds, which exhibited a wide, rainbow effect of colors. The scene would surpass that of a South American rain forest.

Col. Fisher, in a rare moment of emotion exclaimed. "Boys, ain't it beautiful! Hell, it's paradise, just like that Garden Of Eden Delaney is always preaching about!"

Yates and Hall both agreed they had never seen anyplace as beautiful. The day was now drawing to an end. The sun was showing its last dim rays of the light and it was decided that any exploration of the planet would be put off until the next day. In the morning, a pair of Golden Hawks would be launched to perform long range recon missions, while foot and motor patrols would scout out areas closer to the fortress. The three men went back to the ship to map out operations for the following day over chow.

The following morning, at the break of day LCDR Lewis led a recon patrol of three Hawks to scour the terrain that surrounded CONSTELLATION.

"S.C.-1 from morning dove, over," Lewis called to the mother ship.

"Morning dove from S.C.-1 go ahead sir," replied LTJG Lister."

"S.C., you wouldn't believe the scenery out here. This planet has to be one of Mother Nature's best kept secrets. We shot a lot of video and are on our way back. Look's like we really did find paradise. Over."

"Morning dove, its great to hear the news, I'll past it onto the captain. He is down at flight ops. S.C.-1 out," Lister responded.

Lister advised the captain of the patrol's report and that they were returning to the ship. Yates advised that he would wait for the patrols return at the air ops station for the debriefing. He also requested that Commander Edwards and Col. Fisher join him.

LCDR Lewis' patrol returned to the ship without incident. Lewis unloaded the video from the hawks and proceeded to the flight debriefing room to meet with Yates, Edwards and Fisher. The four men viewed the videos and were in awe of the beauty of the planet. The magnificence of the rain forest, with its vast array of meandering rivers and streams covered nearly the entire region surrounding CONSTELLATION.

Commander Edwards remarked, "I can't believe anything could possibly go wrong here. This is a perfect place to ride out the magnetic storm; it's so peaceful, an ideal sanctuary."

Col. Fisher commented on Edwards' statement. "When you think everything is just right and harms way is miles off, that's when it will sneak up on you. I just have a sneaking suspicion something nasty could be lurking in the shadows or off in the mist on this paradise. Just be cautious, my friends."

Yates added to the conversation, "Sam, you just may have a point here. Let's not take all this tranquility without a grain of salt. We need to keep our guard up."

Fisher then stated, "Al, I'm with you. Please excuse me, I have to check in with Captain Webb. He is readying a surface patrol of the area. I'll catch up with you boys in a while." Fisher then left to meet with the out-going patrol.

LCDR Lewis asked, "Captain, I'd like to take a second air recon mission down to the south. There is a valley down there that looks pretty as hell. It's well worth a second look."

Yates replied, "That might not be a bad idea, I think the army is scouting down to the south. They may appreciate a bird in the air. Go ahead and chow down first, then head out. You may want to advise

Col. Fisher and Captain Webb that you'll be in the area."

Lewis headed out to converse with his army counterparts as Yates and Edwards started towards the officer's mess for some coffee. As they were walking through the corridor they saw Ensign Washington stepping out of what they thought was an empty storage compartment. He entered the passageway and paused, unaware that his movements were being observed. Washington was grinning widely, and he rubbed his hands together as if he were up to something mischievous. He turned to lock the compartment door, then started down the corridor towards the captain and the X.O. When he saw the two gold braid officers, he quickly did an about-face, with the pretense of not seeing them.

Captain Yates ordered, "Halt mister, about face and stand fast!"

Washington immediately stopped in his tracks and turned around. Yates and Edwards walked up to him and studied him with curiosity.

Commander Edwards then inquired, "Why Mister Washington, you seem to be up to something. You seem just a little jittery, and why would that be?"

Washington replied, "Nothing sir, I was just down here checkin' on some repairs that my boys done. You know, it's hard to get good talented crackers these days. Sheet, I always gots to check up on dees boys. And how are you two sirs doing on this fine, fine day? We sure do has us one fine paradise planet out there, don't we. Hell, I was just on my way back to my quarters to put on some shorts and get outside and soak up some rays. Hell, it looks fine, so peaceful and everything. I just can't wait to….."

Captain Yates stopped him in mid sentence. "Why Tyrone, my man, I'm so proud of you checking up on the repairs in this section. You are right on the ball, setting a fine example for everyone on this ship to follow. However, you signed off on them last night. I must ask you this, what the hell are you up to?"

Washington then stammered, "I,.. I did? Oh, that's right. Sheet, I must have forgotten. Silly me. Well I guess I'll be getting some rays, see you sirs later."

Commander Edwards then jumped in. "Tyrone, my friend let's not be in such a rush. Since the three of us are here, let's go in and inspect the fine work you and your men have done."

Washington was now quite nervous and was scratching his head. "Sirs, hell. There ain't no need for that. You guys are busy. Trust me, everything is ship shape."

Yates then said, "Trust me? Hell, if that isn't the biggest clue that you're up to something I don't know what is. Now open the door mister. THAT IS AN ORDER!"

Ensign Washington slowly obeyed the captain's order. As soon as the door was unlocked and opened, Yates and Edwards peered inside, and as they did, both their jaws dropped wide open. Inside the compartment was a big red, white and blue banner reading **TYRONE'S PALACE**, slot machines and gaming tables stretched wall to wall.

Commander Edwards said, "Tyrone, you amaze me, you simply amaze me. What the hell are you doing in here?"

The three men walked to the center of the room and looked around. They noticed a computer sitting on a table in the corner. Edwards walked over to it and looked at the screen. It contained a list of crewmen, who apparently owed money to the makeshift casino. He blurted out, "Holy Shit, these are markers. You can't do this!"

Washington trying to cover up his dastardly enterprise quickly said, "Markers, sheet no sir. I took it upon myself to be a morale officer and also to try and teach the younger crewmembers the evils of gambling. Hell, those things are a…a… a teaching aid. Hell, if those boys were in a real casino they would be owing lots of money to those bastards. No sir, you have it all wrong, I'm just looking out for my shipmates."

Yates, hardly keeping a straight face replied, "Tyrone, cut the shit, I wasn't born yesterday. I have to give you an "E" for effort on this one. Now tell me something, what do you use for coins in the slots?"

Before Washington could answer, Commander Edwards walked over to one of the slot machines and gave it a good swift kick. Two coins fell into the tray and were engraved with '.25 cents - THIS BE A WASHINGTON QUARTER'. Edwards picked up one of the coins and turned it over and burst out laughing. "Oh my god captain, look at this." He tossed the coin over to Yates and Yates burst out laughing. The other side of the coin had the face of Washington grinning ear to ear, wearing a tux and a bow tie.

Yates stated, "Tyrone, Tyrone, guess what! Since you appointed yourself morale officer, I'm going to make it official. You now have a new job added to your list of duties. Your casino is now non-profit. Rip up those markers."

The captain was interrupted by Commander Edwards, "Al, look at this. He's got a bar in here too. My god, if we were back in Norfolk you'd be hung from the mast and then flogged."

The captain shook his head in disbelief. He walked over to Washington and put his arm around his shoulder and said in a soft voice, "Mister Washington, when you do things, you do them well. As I was saying before, as the new morale officer you will be working closely with Father Delaney. I will advise him that he should be expecting a visit from you in the very, very near future. That, my son, is another order."

Washington replied in a sheepish voice, "Sir, me and the holy dude really don't see eye to eye. Maybe I could work with someone else who is a little more worldly. That would be better. May I suggest....."

"No, you may not suggest. Lock this place up until you hear back from me. Dismissed."

Yates and Edwards left to complete their trip to the officer's mess. Neither of them could contain their laughter. Yates and Edwards talked about the escapades of Washington over coffee. The captain noticed LCDR Wang, Ensign King and LT. Marsh just leaving the serving line. He motioned to them to join himself and the X.O. They came over to the table and sat down. The conversation turned to how beautiful the planet was, then LCDR Wang commented to the captain.

"Sir, Ensign King and I were on the observation deck yesterday afternoon and noticed what appeared to be ruins just outside the compound. We wondered if they could possibly be the remains of a civilization that inhabited this planet some time ago. With your permission, we would like to go and check it out. Lt Marsh has volunteered to accompany us as an armed escort."

"Is that true Lt Marsh, you would be willing to lay your life down in defense of these two ladies?" The captain asked.

"Why yes sir, I have always been very interested in science and wish to extend any assistance to the science department, in any capacity," Marsh answered, with a reddening face.

"Ensign King, and what would your studies be?" Edwards asked.

"Sir, I would like to check on the foliage to see if it might be of any benefit to us while we are in space." King answered.

"I see no problem, just don't go out to far and get your selves lost. Be careful out there. LCDR Wang is in command of this science expedition, however, their safety is in your hands, Lieutenant," Yates stated.

After finishing coffee, the five left the officers mess. Yates went back to his cabin, Edwards went up to the bridge to start his watch, and Wang, King and Marsh headed out to explore the ruins. As they left the compound they saw the tail end of Captain Webb's convoy heading south in the distance.

Webb's convoy consisted of four humvees containing five men each. Two of the vehicles had 20 caliber machine guns mounted on the roofs. Webb decided to follow the river that flowed south, just off to the west side of the compound. The morning was bright and sunny with just a hint of a breeze that made it comfortable to travel. The atmosphere of the soldiers traveling through the prolific rain forest put everyone at ease. They were joking with each other, throwing all caution to the wind, not having a care in the world. The movement of the convoy was slow at times due to fallen trees and other natural obstacles that impeded travel.

Webb noticed a clearing up ahead and advised his driver they would take a break there to stretch their legs and do some snooping around. As they pulled into the clearing they noticed tall grasses to the east that led up to small foothills that contained numerous caves. About a hundred yards to the west of the clearing, the river flowed with a soft current. Trees of various sizes and colors dipped their foliage into the sparkling water. It was a postcard picture, a perfect place to rest.

Wang, King and Marsh made their way to the ruins and began investigating.

Ensign King noticed some plants that seemed to be bearing a small fruit or some kind of vegetable by a pool of water. She went over to examine it. LT. Marsh was helping to move a large stone for

LCDR Wang, and neither noticed that King had wandered away from the ruin site. King dug up several of the plants from the shore line of a small pond and placed them into her haversack. She stood up and was ready to head back to Wang and Marsh. As she turned and took her first step, a large tentacle darted up from a concealed hole that was covered with dry grass and wrapped around her leg. She screamed from pain and fright as she was being pulled into the hole. Wang and Marsh jumped up to see what was happening and called out for King.

King could be heard yelling, "HELP, HELP, HELP."

They located her and ran towards her cries. Marsh was taking his sidearm out of its holster as he ran. They reached King just as she was pulled half way down into the hole.

"Hang on Barb, we got you, just hold on," Marsh screamed.

"Hold on honey, we'll help you, grab onto our hands," Wang yelled.

Marsh and Wang tried to pull her free, but the tentacle was fighting to drag her down. Her leg was bleeding profusely and an odorous, toxic substance oozed into the wounds from the tentacle's suction-like grip. Marsh was finally able to get a clear shot at the slimy arm and managed to get several rounds into it, forcing it to loose its hold. Marsh holstered his weapon and assisted Wang in pulling Ensign King to safety. King was squirming with pain and was starting to loose consciousness. LCDR Wang started to treat her wounds the best she could while trying to calm King down.

"Just hold on a little longer, we will get some help. You're going to be fine." Then she looked up to LT. Marsh and asked, "How in the hell are we going to get her back to the ship?"

"Don't worry ma'am, I'll carry her," Marsh said.

COL Fisher was up on the southern embankment inspecting one of the gun placements when he heard the commotion. He looked up to see what was happening and recognized trouble. He jumped down onto an M-1 Abrams Battle Tank and ordered the crew to head to the ruins. He grabbed the radio set as the iron horse got underway and notified CONSTELLATION.

"Constellation, Constellation this is Bravo Six. Over."

"Bravo Six, this is Constellation, LTJG Lister. Over."

"LT., this is Col Fisher. We heard some yelling and gunshots coming from the ruins. I have one of my M-1's fired up and we are heading towards them. Don't know what's happening, but it didn't sound good. Over."

"I roger that, sir. I'll notify Commander Edwards. Constellation out."

The news of the event was passed onto the Commander and he thought to himself, "My god, are we under attack?" Edwards looked over to LCDR Hall, who was checking out the status of repairs on the weapons consol and said,

"Randy, looks like someone or something may be raining on our parade. Bring CONSTELLATION to battle stations."

LCDR Hall acknowledged the order and the ship echoed the alarm WHOOP, WHOOP, WHOOP. "ALL HANDS MAN YOUR BATTLE STATIONS. THIS IS NOT A DRILL!" All stations reported ready within seconds. Captain Yates called up to the bridge to see what was happening. He was informed of the incident he then rushed to the bridge.

LCDR Lewis heard the radio traffic and turned his air patrol around to provide air support, if it became necessary. Captain Webb and his patrol were eating lunch when they saw the three Golden

Hawks rushing north. One of his men jumped and exclaimed,

"Damn, look at those fuckers go. Shit, they're in a strike formation. What's going on?"

Captain Webb ordered his radio operator to contact the ship and ascertain the cause for alarm.

LCDR Wang did what she could for the stricken young ensign, who by now had passed out. Marsh picked her up and he and the Lieutenant Commander started walking back to CONSTELLATION at a hurried pace. They had walked about 400 yards when the M-1 Abrams popped up over the hill and stopped in front of them. Col Fisher jumped off the tank and helped LT Marsh carry King to the iron war horse.

"What happened, how bad is she?" Fisher asked.

LCDR Wang gave him the specifics of the incident. Fisher radioed the ship and advised them to have medical teams standing by on the hanger deck. The M-1, with all on board headed back at top speed. The tank roared through the impoundment right up the ramp into the hanger deck. Yates and Dr. Jagman were waiting for them. As soon as the young ensign was lowered from the tank she was placed onto a litter and rushed up to sick bay.

The ship stood down from battle stations and the information about the incident was passed along to all patrols still out in the field.

It was touch and go for a while in sick bay, but finally an antitoxin was found, and Ensign King regained consciousness. Her leg was badly torn and required a considerable amount of stitches to repair. Captain Yates, Fisher, Wang, and LT Marsh were standing by King's bed.

"How do you feel ensign, do you remember what happened?"

Yates asked.

The young ensign, still a little groggy replied, "Oh, I guess I'm o.k. I was getting some specimens and this great big snake bit me. It tried to eat me captain, it really did. LT Marsh saved me, he's my hero."

The red-faced lieutenant stood uneasily as his superiors glanced at him, almost as if they had just realized there might be some involvement between the young lieutenant and the ensign.

The radio operator advised Captain Webb that the holes covered by dead foliage contained some kind of a beast and caution should be used while on foot. Webb advised his command of the hazard.

It was mid afternoon when the patrol completed its recon of the area. Nothing interesting was found; however, an absence of wild life close to the river was noted. Webb noticed that the sky was starting to cloud up so he ordered his men to pack things up and head back to the ship. The convoy turned around and started north. A light mist started to fall, gradually turning to rain. The wet condition slowed down travel. The soil was rapidly becoming saturated and the humvee's started to slide and sink in the mud.

The patrol was just crossing a small stream when the last vehicle became bogged down in the mud. The black ooze covered it up to the running board.

The rain started to let up and the soldiers got on each side and behind the humvee, managing to push it out of the stream bed to higher ground, rejoining the rest of the convoy.

The task of cleaning the encrusted mud from the undercarriage was tedious and time consuming. It was starting to get late and the first signs of darkness were starting to creep in. Webb wanted to make it back to the ship well before nightfall. He ordered his men to get underway, but one soldier spoke up,

"Captain, I gotta take a leak, can you hold off for a second?"

Webb replied, "O.K., but make it snappy and remember more than two shakes is pleasure."

The soldier walked towards a clump of trees by the river so he could perform his duty with some privacy. He disappeared behind a tree, all the time being jeered by his comrades. A horrific scream came from where the soldier hid himself. The men grabbed their weapons and charged towards the trees, only find the corpse of their friend torn apart, lying in a pool of blood. His guts were strewn about, hanging in the blood covered bushes. Webb noticed a trail of slime heading towards the river and ordered,

"O.K. men, look sharp. Let's find the bastard that done this to Brent."

The patrol slowly followed the trail of slime. They heard some rustling in the bushes in front of them. As they peeled back the brush, they saw a terrifying sight - a large creature stood ten feet tall, gray in color, with long arms that ended in twelve inch long razor sharp claws. Below the arms were tentacles that contained patches of sharp pin-like stingers filled with venom. The head was that of a devil, and the rest of the body looked like an over grown slug. The creature turned around and started to attack the soldiers. It captured one man in its tentacle, leaving him paralyzed and picked him up with its massive arms. It slashed its victim, spraying blood on everyone and everything. Webb and his men fired at the beast, but it did not stop the beast from tearing into its prey. The man screamed out in agony each time the slug-devil bit a hunk of flesh from its blood covered meal, finally putting the man out of his misery as it swallowed his head.

One soldier ran back to the vehicle and returned with an R.P.G. As he was readying the weapon, the slug-devil advanced towards the retreating patrol. The beast slapped its tentacle onto a third victim and opened its mouth with a thunderous roar. The open mouth proved to be its mistake, as the rocket-propelled grenade found the blood frothed opening a perfect target, exploding on impact, shattering the skull into a hundred blood-covered bits, ending the skirmish.

Captain Webb and his men carried the stricken soldier back to the humvees and performed what first aid they could. CONSTELLATION was contacted and advised of the encounter. Yates ordered one of the transports to be launched to transport the injured man back to the ship for treatment. The airlift completed, the convoy proceeded back to compound and secured from the patrol that had left two dead and one critically wounded. Captain Webb met with Captain Yates and Col. Fisher and gave a report on the incident. Webb made a point of his observation that the area around the river showed no signs of wildlife, as compared to the rest of the forest. Perhaps the humans were now to be a new food source for the creatures.

Yates advised, "We have two dead, two recovering in sickbay. As of right now, no one goes out alone or leaves the compound alone for any reason."

Fisher agreed and the order was posted. The creature, now known as the slug-devil, was a ruthless killing machine. After studying the reports of both incidents, it was determined that the creature lived by water. It would move on the ground during times of high moisture, rain, or shortly after a rain storm. With this information, troops on patrol would be better able to protect themselves against the ravishing beast.

The air operations weather section had advised the command staff that they could expect several days of rain. With this forecast in hand, Colonel Fisher ordered the guards to be doubled on the fortress embankments and for flood lights to be installed to illuminate the area outside the compound. The rainy weather would be prime time for movement of the slug-devil.

As forecasted, the rain moved in, at times a downpour, but for the most part it was a light mist with patches of fog. Yates, Fisher, Edwards and Major Kinkaid were meeting in the bridge conference room, discussing the turn of events. The planet once considered a paradise was now becoming a bloody nightmare.

"Sam, I understand you have upgraded security around the ship. Is there anything else you need?" Captain Yates inquired.

"I think things are copasetic for the time being. LCDR Hall is working pretty closely with me on this," Col Fisher replied.

"Colonel Fisher, I can't help but remember you saying that something in the shadows would sneak up and bite us, or something like that. By god you were right on this one." Commander Edwards commented.

"Yes I did, I'm sorry that it came true. I was just starting to like this place. Hell, I was thinking about moving here when I retire," Fisher jokingly responded.

Captain Yates turned to Major Kinkaid and asked, "Brian, do you have any suggestions or comments on our security measures?"

"No, there's not really anything further to do. I chatted with LT Atkins about a rotation schedule due to the dampness and chill of the night air and he worked up a plan of action. Four hours on, eight hours off. I also had the mess bring down a few coffeepots. Ensign Washington rigged up power for them, so the boys on the line have a fresh supply of hot java when they want it. I do have a question about Washington. He said that since "US" army boys are doing a fair job defending the ship, he was only going to charge ten cents a cup. What's up with that guy?"

Everyone in the room chuckled and Commander Edwards commented.

"No, major, it's WAZZUP with that guy. Mr. Washington is always looking for a way to make a buck. The only thing you have to say to him when he acts up is, "Father Delaney is looking for you."

The meeting came to an end and the officers went their separate ways. Yates was headed back to his quarters when he ran into Commander Jagman.

"Doctor, how are our two patients doing?" Yates asked

"SGT Royce is stable. He is still out of it yet for the most part. Ensign King was released a few hours ago. I want her on bed rest for a week. My staff will be checking in on her several times a shift. I am questioning if they really do need to check up on her though," Jagman replied.

"What do you mean by that doctor?" Yates asked.

"Well, it seems she is in good hands. LT Marsh is taking good care of her. As much as he seems to be playing doctor, perhaps he should be re-assigned to the medical unit," the doctor elaborated.

"I see, maybe I should check this care provider thing out," Yates joked. "Have a pleasant evening and keep COL Fisher and myself updated on SGT Royce's condition."

Jagman assured the captain he would keep them both informed; the two men then returned to their business.

The outside temperature had now dipped into the low fifties the fog had grown thicker. Visibility was down to seventy-five yards. The sentries were growing weary from eye strain as they kept a careful lookout for the slug-devil.

Two guards at the far end of the compound thought they heard something moving around at the base of the fortification.

"Pete, did you hear that?" Private Abby asked.

"Yeah, I don't know where it came from. I don't see anything. I'm going down to take a look, cover me," Private Noon replied.

Noon left his post and slowly made his way down to the bottom of the embankment, as his partner kept him in sight.

"Hey Mat, I don't see anything. I'm just gonna check around the corner here, then I'll be back up."

Private Abby said O.K., and told him to be careful. Then he heard a roar and an agonizing scream.

"Pete, Pete are you O.K?" Abby called into the darkness, only to be met by a chilling silence. "Pete, where are you?"

Private Abby started down to check on his partner. He slipped down the muddy fortress wall and found himself covered in blood. "SHIT" he exclaimed. He got back on his feet and crept around the corner and stood face to face with a slug-devil. He started shooting his weapon, but to no avail. The beast lifted him up and started to devour him alive. His life-sustaining blood gushed out of his body with every bite of torn flesh.

The commotion drew the attention of the remaining sentries, and soon the muzzle flash of the M-16's and machine guns lit up the thick fog. The incident was reported to the bridge and CONSTELLATION was called to battle stations.

Reports of additional slugs soon reached the commanders and additional troops were sent out to battle the beasts. The slug-devils had tunneled underneath the fortification mounds and were inside the compound. The fight was one that had never been experienced by the crew. It was both horrifying and terrifying as human limbs were torn from the fighters and tossed in every direction. Pools of warm blood settled everywhere. The defenders couldn't tell if it were rain or blood that was soaking their uniforms.

Several men were hit by friendly fire as their panic turned into utter chaos. Lead projectiles flew in every direction. For a period of time, all defense measures seemed to have failed. In a last ditch effort to keep the creatures of evil from entering the ship, COL. Fisher rigged up flame throwers. As the first creature slid its way up the ramp into the ship, it was met by a stream of blazing fire. It let out an ear-piercing wail and collapsed in a ball of flames, rolling off of the ramp into the blood stained mud.

Additional flame throwers were deployed, and one by one the beasts fell into smoldering heaps, bursting open and spewing their guts of half-digested human parts through the air, draping the CONSTELLATION with a thick, red, slimy ooze.

As the first rays of the sun crept into the morning sky, the slug-devils slithered back into the safety of their holes in the floor of the rain forest. The clean up of the compound began. Total casualties for the night were twelve dead and thirty-two wounded. It was the worst battle losses suffered by the earthlings to date.

Captain Yates called for a meeting of his combat commanders in the deck six conference room. One by one the officers, soiled and stained with blood, reported for the meeting.

Yates opened the gathering with a poignant statement, "Gentlemen, we were hit hard last night. The losses we suffered can't go on. We have no way to get replacement personnel. These slug-devils, as they are called, are not only deadly as we have found, but they also seem to be able to communicate with each other. The attack last night was not just a herd of animals gathering for a hunt, it was a coordinated effort. They are crafty. They attacked on the surface and tunneled under ground. They assault their prey at night, using poor visibility and weather conditions to their advantage. How can we combat this?"

Colonel Fisher interjected his observations. "If we send out patrols on the ground, they will be massacred. The creatures attacked the fortress in mass, rendering our air power and iron horses useless. We can't bombard our own house. If we could get them to mass out in the open, we could blow them to kingdom come. Unlike us they are still able to get replacements. I think our best bet would be to bulldoze a killing field around the outside perimeter. That would at least give us a clear shot at them with the big guns when they attack."

Major Kinkaid added to the brainstorming, "I noticed last night that the most effective weapon was the flame thrower. Perhaps we could rig some high-powered ones on a few of the Bradleys. The flame throwers could be used inside the compound or out in the field."

"Lieutenant Williams, can you give us an update on the magnetic storm?" Captain Yates asked.

"Sir, it looks like the storm may be entering its final phase. The readings over the past couple of days have showed that the magnitudes of the waves themselves are holding steady, and I have noticed a small decrease this morning. In about four to five days it should be fairly safe for flight, if we head away from the source. It still may be a rough ride though," Williams replied.

"It seems we have to stay in this *Paradise Lost* for another week. We came in hard and we were lucky not to crash on landing. However we will need to build a runway for take off if the rain ever stops long enough for us to work on it."

Commander Edwards suggested, "Al, why don't we kill two birds with one stone. The runway will have to be plowed east to west. Why don't we send out a few extra tanks with blades on them at the same time the runway is being forged and they can doze an area north and south of the ship for a shooting gallery."

"Doug, what's the weather look like?" Yates asked.

"Captain, the radar tells me it will be hot and sunny during daylight and wet and cold at night. The ground is pretty well saturated in the morning hours, but is fairly stable by noon. So at the most, we have five to six hours a day to get the work done," LCDR Lewis replied.

"Al, why don't we finish up here? Kinkaid and myself will personally handle the outfitting of blades on the M-1's and turning the Bradley's into mobile Bar-B-Q pits. Maybe we can leave this vacation resort on time," Fisher stated.

All agreed on the plan of action. The meeting adjourned and soon the foliage around fortress CONSTELLATION was being turned into a killing field that would double as a runway.

The M-1 battle tanks were leveling the earth around Connie as the Bradley's, fitted with high powered flame throwers, patrolled the area. Several Humvee's were outfitted with machine guns and assisted in scouting for the gray beasts as the work was being done.

On the first night the weather forecast was wrong; rain did not appear and that gave way to a longer work day. With no precipitation for over twenty-four hours the ground was fairly dry, making the bulldozing easier. Rain clouds reappeared on the second afternoon. All were dreading what might happen when daylight gave way to darkness.

As feared, a light misty rain began to fall upon CONSTELLATION. The storm's intensity increased, at times leaving pools of water lying all over the landscape. A fog once again engulfed the fortress, leaving visibility poor. Even with the use of flood lights, the sentries could only see half way down the killing fields. The elements for the battle were most definitely on the side of the slug-devils.

The compound, for the most part was quiet; the only sounds to be heard were the rain spattering in the puddles of water and the occasional splashing of footsteps by fellow crewmen bringing warm beverages to their comrades. There was an eerie feeling of foreboding in the air.

Major Kinkaid was checking up on the troops manning the earthen fortifications. He was half way to the far eastern wall when he noticed one of his men at the bottom of the embankment acting strangely.

"What's the problem, soldier?" he asked

"I dunno sir, I keep hearing a strange sound coming from here," the soldier replied, pointing to the ground.

No sooner did he finish his sentence, when a slug-devil popped up from beneath him. The soldier fell and the beast wrapped its tentacles around the man. Kinkaid drew his weapon and fired at the monster, drawing its attention from the fallen soldier. The slug-devil started towards the major, still clutching the soldier in its tentacle grip. Several more of the alien monsters popped up from under the ground within the compound and the sound of gun fire replaced the stillness. CONSTELLATION was now at battle stations and men were pouring out of the ship to fight the intruders. Chaos once again was the order of business. Slug-devils appeared on the horizon and approached the compound, crossing the killing field's deadly spray of bullets.

Kinkaid managed to skirt around the beast and freed the injured soldier from its grasp. As he was trying to pull the man to a safer location, the slug-devil grabbed him with its arm and lifted him up. The major knew this situation would not have a happy ending and continued to empty his weapon into the beast. His efforts were futile as the beast lifted him up higher and higher and finally the major was face to face with the devil. The devil, with one fierce bite took off the major's head. Blood splatter soon turned the small streams of muddy water to red.

Two soldiers who were equipped with flame throwers saw Kinkaid in trouble and rushed the slug-devil, but they were too late. The major was now just a heap of flesh on the ground. As the monster started towards the two men, they opened fire. The beast howled with pain as the fire smothered out every ounce of its life. It collapsed in the mud, smoldering and popping.

The smell of blood had enticed scores of other slug-devils to the area, making this assault upon the earthlings twice the size as the one before. Even with poor visibility, several Hawks managed to take off and proceeded with deadly strafing runs across the killing fields, stopping the carnivorous aggressors in their tracks.

Four Bradley's fitted out with high-powered flame throwers trekked their way through the mud and ooze to attack the devils as they approached the compound. The slug-devils advance was starting to fade as the assault on the compound proving the human race's resolve to survive.

Inside the compound, the battle was at a standstill. The stench of death leached its way into every nook and cranny. Bloody human limbs and organs covered the entire compound area. Horrific screams of pain drowned out the emissive gunfire that was loosed to keep the creatures at bay. Colonel Fisher resorted back to Civil War battlefield tactics, having his men line up in groups of twelve, having the first line fire at their target, emptying their weapons, dropping back to reload while the second line emptied their weapons into the intruders. This tactic proved to be a successful measure. Several of the beasts were destroyed in this way.

The battle lasted into the early hours of the morning, when the slug-devils tried to make their way back into the safety of the forest. Fisher would not permit them to escape. He kept on their tails until the last one floundered on the ground dying.

The storm passed and rays of sun were doing their part to dry up the soil. Yates and Fisher stood in the midst of bloody bodies and limbs, trying to take in the devastation that had occurred that night. Details were organized, first to bring in the wounded and second, to try and sort through the corpses and limbs. Although the rain waters were drying, the soil was slippery from blood and membranes.

All of the sickbay areas of the ship were full of the injured and the dying, Doctor Jagman and his staff were overwhelmed. LCDR Wang and Father Delaney were there, trying to help out the best they could. Medics, exhausted from the night of battle, still administered aid to the fallen.

Yates and Fisher left the blood-drenched compound and headed to the Air Ops station to confer with LCDR Lewis.

"Doug, what is the intensity of the magnetic storm?" Yates asked him.

"Captain, it's still a rough ride up there, but the storm is dissipating. It is going down fast. I think we could ride it out, if that's what you have in mind," Lewis answered.

"That's exactly what I have in mind. Ammo is getting low and we lost too many people. We can't stay here any longer. Check on the weather and get me the condition of the strip. If it's do-able, we will leave this evening."

Lewis and a couple of men went out to investigate the condition of the air strip. The strip was drying up fairly fast in the hot sun. A few pot holes were found from the exploding ordinance from the night before and would need to be filled in.

Lewis caught up with Yates, who by now was on the bridge with Commander Edwards. He gave him his report and Yates ordered Edwards to get preparations underway to launch Connie back into space.

Yates left the bridge and headed to the main sick bay area to talk with Commander Jagman. He found Jagman, who was exhausted leaning up against the bulkhead taking a short break.

"Dave, I know you're trying to take a rest, I'm sorry to disturb you, but how bad are things?" Yates asked.

"Captain, at last count we have thirty dead, twenty-five in real bad shape, and over a hundred wounded. That's just from last night's melee. We are getting real cramped for supplies and room. Washington has dedicated three of the replicators just for medical needs. I don't think we can take another night like this," Jagman replied.

"Doc, we are getting ready to get the hell out of here. It will take several hours before we can taxi out onto the strip. So it may be wise to handle your more serious surgical cases now. It's going to be a rough ride up there."

Jagman took heed of the captain's advice and got all of his surgical teams back on the job.

Col. Fisher and Captain Webb were taking charge of tearing down the earthen fortress and Commander Edwards was directing stowage for the equipment being brought back on board. As the walls of the compound were being dismantled, bloodied limbs were found. A few slug-devils that were trying to hide from the sun's rays were also uncovered and destroyed on the spot.

It was close to sundown when the preparations were completed, and an anxious Captain Yates awaited the final reports on the bridge. All divisions reported ready, the only thing now was the weather. Yates had noticed earlier that thick black clouds were building in the west. This storm could possibly delay Connie's take off.

LCDR Lewis arrived on the bridge and gave the captain his forecast.

"Sir, we have about a ninety minute window for take off, after that, all hell is going to break loose. It's a nasty one coming in."

"Thanks, Doug. I think we better get this show on the road. Commander Edwards, looks like we are going to be taking off into a storm. Make sure everything is battened down and see if Dr. Jagman needs any help. We launch in sixty minutes."

"Al, that's cutting it kind of close isn't it," Edwards asked.

"By the time we back Connie up to the east end of the strip and get everything powered up, that should be about right. We ain't spending another night in this bloody paradise."

Edwards carried out the captain's orders, and soon CONSTELLTION was backed to the farthest reach of the runway. The general alarm sounded for all personnel to man their stations for lift off. The first drops of rain were starting fall on the ship's hull when Yates gave the order. The ship first started to move slowly, then she picked up speed. The runway was starting to show weakness from the rain, causing Connie to swerve several times on the slippery surface. As the nose lifted off the ground a sense of relief could be felt throughout the entire ship. She was airborne, leaving the deadly planet in her wake. CONSTELLATION stayed in a low orbit for several days until the magnetic storm had weakened itself to the point as not to be a threat for a safe flight.

CHAPTER 3

# BACK TO FLOX

CONSTELLATION left the orbit of the planet and headed back into deep space. The atmosphere on board her was one of sorrow - sorrow over the loss of more than fifty crew members and friends from doing battle with the slug-devils. Several of the crew who died in sick bay from wounds inflicted by the slug-devils had been taken to a morgue in the lower holds of the space craft for burial on earth, if CONSTELLATION ever made it home.

The remaining deceased that had been badly torn and mutilated were placed in a large plastic container with one dog tag for each person included. The other tag would be given to the next of kin back on earth.

Once again the hanger deck became a makeshift chapel. Father Delaney led the service with prayer.

"Friends we are gathered here today to pay final tribute to our comrades and friends who have fallen in battle against an evil beast who had to come from the gates of hell itself. These children of the Lord fought bravely against a creature whose only purpose in life was that of feeding itself. There are many stories of gallantry - one that comes to mind is that of Major Brian Kinkaid, United States Army. Major Kinkaid saw that one of his men was about to become the next victim of one of the savage beasts. He pulled the man to safety, sacrificing his own life. May God bless his soul. In our journey we have seen battle with other beings and yes, other beast. But never have the deaths of our friends been so brutal. Rest assured these souls are resting in the bounty of our lord's flock.

We will never forget these men. They will always have a place in our hearts and in our minds. Please step forward and pay your final respects to the departed before we commit their remains into the voids of space for their final rest."

One by one the crew said their goodbyes as bag pipes played Amazing Grace over the P.A. system. The last person passed the collective bodies and gave a final salute. The procession then gathered in the hanger deck observation room and watched as crewmen garbed in space suites gently lifted the bundle into space. LT Marsh was holding Ensign King as she cried on his shoulder. King, who was recovering yet from her wounds was allowed to attend the ceremony. She was still quite weak from her injuries and started to collapse on the deck. LT Marsh carried her back to her quarters. Yates, Fisher and Father Delaney remained in the observation room after the others had left. They watched the container slowly drift away into space.

Fisher, who was showing signs of strain from the deaths of his men, slammed his fist down and said,

"Dammit, Brian was a good man. I should have been out there. Why him, why him? I can't believe he's gone."

Yates grabbed him by the shoulder and said, "Sam, I remember a few weeks ago, you said to me "Don't let it eat you up". Friend, don't let it. It was utter chaos out there that night. You were out there with the rest of us. It's not your fault. I'll be damn glad when this ship returns home."

"Sam, and you too Alex, You both cannot blame yourselves for these losses. We have been placed in the far reaches of the universe, battling creatures of the evilest kind. If not for your leadership abilities the consequences may have been much worst. It is God's grace that you both lead not only with your minds, but also with your hearts. It is an honor to call you both friends." Father Delaney stated.

The hanger deck doors closed and Father Delaney left to help out in sick bay. Yates and Fisher went to Yates' quarters to have a drink and to reflect on the loss of the crewmen who had died.

As they were talking a knock came from the door "It's open, enter." Yates said.

It was LT Williams. "I'm sorry to disturb you sir, but we kind of have a problem."

"What is it?" Yates asked.

"Sir, the magnetic storm or the hot entry on the planet corrupted a lot of navigational search programs. The backups were destroyed when things shorted out. When the ship got hot it cooked most everything. I'm afraid the only way to get things running again would be to return to Flox and have them re-installed," the Lieutenant answered.

"Well, Al that's two reasons now. Malloy is having engine trouble and now this young man has broken his computer. I think I've seen a Best Buy just down the street from Kalgor's house, maybe we can stop in there," Fisher jokingly said.

"Mr. Williams, why weren't the programs stored in the data archives area with the rest of the back ups?" Yates asked.

"Sir, for a while we thought we had glitches in the active program from the magnetic storm. LT. Marsh and my self were re-installing them when all hell broke loose. Errr... Errr...I guess we got caught up in the moment and it slipped our minds," Williams replied.

Just then a second knock came from the door. "Enter," Yates called out. It was Commander Jagman.

"Captain, I hope I'm not interrupting. Could I have a moment of your time?" Jagman asked.

"Yes doctor, what is it?" Yates asked.

"Captain, I have twelve seriously injured men in sickbay. We re-attached limbs that were literally dangling by a thread back onto their bodies. Although our equipment had been modernized on Flox, the damage is too severe for us to handle on board. Even if we amputate arms and legs, I fear some of these men are in danger of losing their lives if we don't get them advanced help real soon" Jagman insisted.

"Well that's three for Flox and zero for deep space," Fisher broke in.

"We have lost enough men; the engines aren't up to snuff, and Lieutenant Williams needs to go to Best Buy - three good reasons to turn around, "Yates replied.

The captain called up to the bridge and ordered the ship be brought on a course that would bring them to the Flox system. The word spread around the ship that they were headed back to friendly territory. This brought a soothing effect to everyone's nerves. The last planet Connie landed on was a deadly horror-filled nightmare.

Yates went down to sick bay to get an updated report on the twelve men. Commander Jagman and LCDR Wang were tending to the wounded. Yates stood back and watched as they changed the dressing on one man's leg. The wound was oozing a dark green thick liquid and the limb itself was bright red and blistered. A foul order emitted from the wound, almost making the captain sick to his stomach. After the leg was cleaned and re-bandaged, the captain went up to the two healers.

"What's the prognosis on these men?" He asked.

"Not good Al. I don't know how long we can keep them going, even on life support. I saw you come in so I know you have seen the wounds. That green ooze is venom from the slug-devils. These guys had so much injected into them that the anti toxin is hardly combating it at all. It is imperative that we reach the medical facilities on Flox as soon as possible," Jagman replied.

"Captain, we have tried transfusions and everything. The crew has been very generous in donating blood, but for some reason it's not helping," LCDR Wang injected.

"Are you sure they will recover if we get them to Flox?" Yates asked

"They will have a better chance. We are doing all we can here, buts it's not enough. They have no chance at all if we don't reach a better equipped facility, captain," Jagman stated.

Yates walked over to a phone in the ward and called up to the bridge.

"Ralf, check with Malloy, see how long we can run at flank speed. Fisher's men in sick bay are getting worse. If we don't make it to Flox real soon we are going to start to loose them."

Within a few minutes the ship shuttered as the CONSTELLATION strained to gain speed. The ship would run flat out for two hours and then drop down to three-quarters speed, switching back and forth as not to put too much of a strain on the engines. Yates asked the medics to inform him of any changes in the men's condition.

Yates went up to the bridge and conferred with Commander Edwards.

"Ralf, how far are we from Flox?"

"About six days away captain, at current speeds. Malloy advised that if we push the engines any harder something might blow," Edwards replied.

"LTJG Lister, are we in communications range of Flox yet?" Yates asked.

"No sir, we should be in range within the next thirty-six hours. I will try to raise the Flox Military Tactical Command Center every hour, just in case we get lucky,"

Lister replied.

"Very well, thank you lieutenant," Yates concluded.

Yates relieved Edwards of the watch. Edwards was heading back down to his quarters, when he heard some giggling and laughter. As he turned the corner, he found LT Marsh and ENS King passionately embracing in the doorway to King's quarters.

"Ah-hmm, and how are we doing this fine evening, children?" Edwards asked.

The two lovers were startled and jumped apart. The embarrassed Lt then replied, "Oh, just fine sir. I was just helping Ensign King unbutton her, I mean helping her with the door. It seemed to be jammed."

Commander Edwards, giving them a skeptical look, commented, "Perhaps we need to get a repair party up here to look at it - no, let me see if I can help out."

"Oh, no need to do so sir, I have things well in hand," Marsh hastily snapped back.

"Yes, I see that you do, good night, and carry on. Wait, strike that last order," Edwards chuckled.

The X.O. left the area and the two love birds, laughing over being caught, went into King's quarters.

Meanwhile, back on the bridge Captain Yates was studying the star charts to see if there was a way to shave any time off the journey. He was unable to find a short cut.

"LT Lister, any luck raising the Flox Tactical Command yet?" he asked.

"No sir, we are still too far out," she replied.

The captain slammed his fist down on the arm of his chair and was about to speak when a loud GONG, GONG, GONG blared over the ship's P.A. system. "Security to deck H-7, security to deck H-7, security to d – AAAAAAHHHHHHH"

Yates jumped up out of his chair and yelled, "What the hell was that? LCDR Hall to deck H-7."

The captain turned the command over to LCDR Malloy, who had just entered the bridge. Yates ran to the elevator to take it down to the source of the distress. As he arrived at H-7 he met up with LCDR Hall, who was with Commander Edwards. Col Fisher immediately joined up with them.

"What's going on Al? What the hell was that scream?" Fisher asked.

"I don't know, we didn't even get a section number, just deck H-7," Yates replied.

The four officers were now joined by several security detail personnel, and they cautiously proceeded to investigate the area. There was a familiar stench emitting from the passage way just in front of them.

"Captain, over here," LCDR Hall called out.

The deck was covered with a slimy substance, and a dreaded vision of the slug-devils flashed into their minds. The team inched forward, and discovered a pool of blood that covered the deck tile from bulkhead to bulkhead. The entire area was splattered with the red liquid, and as they rounded the corner, they stared in horror at an oozing, severed leg lying on the deck.

"Shit, we have one of those fucking slugs on board!" Yates shouted. "Sam, can you get some of your men down here with flame throwers? Randy, get extra men down here, I want decks 3,4,5,6, and 7 sealed off."

Yates' orders were followed to a tee, the decks that he requested secured were quickly sealed off. Army personnel armed with flame throwers were now in the area hunting for the dreaded slug-devil. One by one, reports came to the captain that the decks in question were safe and secure from the demon that had terrorized CONSTELLATION'S crew on the planet behind them. The security crews converged on deck H-7. The search teams started from the outermost region of the deck and worked their way in, hoping to trap the beast in the center of the deck, killing it in the crossfire. Deck H-7 was a storage deck and had more compartments than any of the other decks. Many of the compartments were elbow-shaped or consisted of several smaller rooms. The search was slow going because of the maze like setting. The entire deck was searched and nothing was found. The security details on the other decks were ordered to re-search their areas to see if they had missed the beast or if it had somehow escaped deck H-7.

Each deck reported back negative. Yates and his fellow officers were stumped.

"Where can that bastard be?" Yates thought out loud, when he noticed a small drop of slime by his feet. As he looked up, another drop fell from the ventilation shaft.

"Up there, toast that mother fucker with everything you got," Yates yelled.

The flame throwers brightly lit up the corridor, which reverberated with the sound of M-16 assault rifles. An ear-piercing screech resounded from within the overhead shaft. The metal melted from the intense heat of the flame throwers and began to weaken. The section gave way and the creature plummeted to the deck with a loud THUD. The burning body of the beast started to bloat and exploded with a hiss, covering the men and corridor with slime and stench. The order to cease fire was given as the slug-devil lay on its back with a gaping hole in its stomach. The bewildered men peered into the beast cavity; they could make out the partially digested remains of the crewman that had called for help.

What was left of the crewman was taken to the ship's morgue and the devil was sent to an icy tomb in space. Yates ordered LCDR Hall to have security details search the entire ship to ascertain if any more of the devils had made it aboard.

With the emergency over, Yates went back to his quarters to change into a fresh uniform before he returned to the bridge. Yates relieved Malloy and took over the watch. He asked LTJG Lister if there were any change in the status of communications with the Flox. She advised no change.

Commander Jagman and LCDR Wang were holding a constant vigil over the wounded men. Their frustrations were running high as there seemed to be no immediate relief for the gallant warriors. The only hope for recovery was the medical centers of Flox, if only they could make it there in time.

"Dave, you've been up constantly with these men, why don't you get some rest. There is nothing we can do for them at this point," LCDR Wang conveyed to him.

"Laura, I know that you are right, but it just seems like there is something we are missing. I've gone over the treatments a thousand times in my head and I just can't seem to put my finger on it. I have to do something, I just can't let them lay there and die," Jagman responded.

"The captain will get us there in time, I'm confident about that. Get some sleep you're dead on your feet. If there are any changes I'll call you," Wang advised.

The doctor left sick bay and headed towards his quarters. He decided to stop off at the officer's mess for a quick cup of coffee and noticed Father Delaney sitting alone at a table.

"Good evening Father, mind if I join you?" Jagman asked.

"Why no, sit down. Looks like you're pretty worried. Is there anything I can help you with?" Delaney inquired.

"No, I'm just troubled over the lack of response I'm getting from the men in sick bay. I fear we may loose them. I have tried everything in the book and the results are still the same. I am at a loss for an answer," Doctor Jagman replied.

"Doctor, sip your coffee slowly, I have a lot to say. You are a healer, a man of many talents that were crafted by God. The Lord has the final say of who lives and who dies. Do not carry that burden on your shoulders. Keep the faith in the Lord. He will guide your hands. I know that you have been up day and night with the ill. Don't wear yourself down. I know it's hard to understand science and religion, but it's through our faith in God that gives us the tools to help others. I guess in other words, I'll put it in navy terms, you have to know when to give up the ship. If you don't, you'll go to Davy Jones's locker with her," Delaney intoned.

Jagman looked the man of the cloth right in his eyes and said, "Father, I know you are correct, but I somehow have to keep trying. That's my job. I am a religious man, I know why God put me on this earth, or should I say this ship. It is to help those who need healing."

The two men finished their coffee and parted ways. Jagman went to his quarters and Delaney went to the ship's main hospital to help out in any way he could.

Captain Yates, still standing watch on the bridge was showing more frustration by not being able to make radio contact with the Flox. He came up with an idea. He got on the ships P.A. system and called for Ensign Washington.

Washington arrived on the bridge. "Yo rang sir, and how may I be of assistance to you captain my main man?"

"Tyrone, my master of deception, I need you to channel all of your wayward abilities to boost our radio signal. If you succeed with this task, I will allow you to keep your casino, however, they will be PENNY SLOTS," the captain said.

"PENNY SLOTS, sheet, I'll have to think about that one. Hell, ain't no money in pennies. How do you expect me to make an honest living?" Washington whined. As he started to say more, the captain shot in.

"You heard me, PENNY SLOTS, and I'll let you keep the bar. Now, can you boost the signal?"

"Now that I'm back in business, sho thing cappytan. I'll have us in contact with those foxy Flox and have us dates lined up in no time. And it won't cost you a dime, to have us a good time," Washington rhymed.

Washington delved right into the project. He tore open the communications consol and fed wires over to the search center. He called down to engineering and requested the necessary parts. The captain and bridge crew watched him with great curiosity as he worked and swore, sparks flying everywhere.

"Shit, oohh that's hot, ouch that fucker hurt," echoed throughout the bridge from Washington.

"Yo, LTJG Lister, try calling the FLOXY brothers and sistas", Washington voiced.

Lister looked over to the captain and Yates nodded his head in agreement.

"Flox Tactical Command Center, this is the USS CONSTELLATION. Over," Lister called. She repeated the hail two more times with no response. Again she hail the flox and was finally rewarded with the response, "USS CONSTELLATION, this is Flox Tactical Command Center on Flox-2. Go ahead with your transmission."

Captain Yates was elated. He advised what had happened and the critical need of assistance for the maimed soldiers in sick bay. The Flox advised they would, in an effort to save crucial time send a science ship to rendezvous with CONSTELLATION. Dr. Jagman was awakened and told of the good news. He proceeded back to the sick bay area to exchange medical data with his Flox counterparts via a special radio patch.

The luck of CONSTELLATION was changing again, this time for the better. As promised, the Flox Tactical Command sent a ship to help with the injured. The Flox Science Ship MALLAR was equipped with a hospital unit that would rival those of her home planet. Dr. Jagman now had great expectations that his patients would soon have the chance they needed to be healed.

The two ships met and both halted their forward momentum. Several shuttle craft from the MALLAR were launched and landed on the hanger deck aboard CONSTELLATION. Crewmen from both worlds hurriedly brought the needed medical supplies to Connie's sick bay to help treat the injured. The plan was to stabilize the men, then transport them to the MALLAR and then on to Flox-2. CONSTELLATION would follow behind.

Within three and a half days, the CONSTELLATION and MALLAR landed on Flox-2. The twelve men were transported to a hospital in the city of Fleddes, their condition was upgraded from near death to critical.

Kalgor greeted his old friends from earth and they discussed the latest adventure, indeed a fatal one. Captain Yates granted shore leave to the entire crew as a reward for their gallant efforts at their last port of call. With a rested and revitalized crew, work would soon begin on the needed repairs aboard CONSTELLATION.

CHAPTER 4

# ON THE ROAD AGAIN

The last of the provisions were being loaded aboard CONSTELLATION and final checks on the recent repairs were underway. Captain Yates and Kalgor were standing in the shadow of the NEOS observing the crews at work.

The ship's complement had all returned from leave, except for Dr. Jagman and LCDR Wang who were at the Flox Medical Facility assisting the twelve soldiers, who had made a complete recovery. They were all getting ready for the trip back to the ship.

Four Hummers arrived at the Tactical Command Base and drove up the ramp into the hanger bay. Jagman and Wang, along with the soldiers had made it back. It was time to get Connie back up in space.

Kalgor and Yates were saying farewell to each other, Kalgor had some parting words.

"Alex, my friend, as you have found out, things are not always what they appear to be. Be wary in your travels in this part of the universe. Remember, you and your fellow earthmen are strangers here and there are a lot of unknowns that can be quite deceptive. I wish we could assist you more with your quest of getting back to earth. Perhaps your journey will be fulfilled in good time."

"Yes, we have learned a hard lesson. One we will never forget. We thank you for your courtesies and help.  Your face is a safe haven in this harsh, perilous part of the universe. I do hope we meet again. Farewell my friend," Yates replied.

The two leaders shook hands and Yates walked up the ramp into the ship. He made his way up to the bridge and inquired about the ships status.

"Commander Edwards, is CONSTELLATION ready for flight?"

"Yes sir, the ramp has been raised and the hanger deck is pressurized. All departments report ready. What are your orders, sir?" Edwards asked.

"Bring CONSTELLATION about, then take us out. Out into space.  Perhaps this time we will find a way home," Yates replied.

"Aye sir, helm come about 1-8-0 degrees, bring all engines on line and take us up," Commander Edwards ordered.

CONSTELLATION slowly swung around and positioned herself on the runway. She crept forward and then gained speed. Within seconds her nose lifted off the ground and she was in flight. The landing gear retracted back into her wings and fuselage and her speed increased. The gigantic star cruiser left the planet's atmosphere as the Flox system melted into the blackness of space, finally becoming sparkling specks dotting the vast cosmos, replacing the planets of the solar system.

Life aboard the cruiser fell back into the daily routines. The Search Center was actively scanning the horizon for any sign of a wormhole that would help them attain their ultimate goal of reaching earth.

With all systems reporting normal, Yates turned the command over to Edwards. He left the bridge and headed to the officer's mess for some coffee. He saw Commander Jagman and COL Fisher sitting together talking. He proceeded over to their table.

"Gentlemen, mind if I join you?"

"Not at all, grab yourself a seat Al," Fisher replied.

"What's the hot topic of discussion?" Yates inquired.

Jagman replied, "We were just chatting about the Flox people and how fortunate we are to have them as allies. Their medical technology is far more advanced than ours. Fisher's men will be up to full speed in no time. I was just telling Sam that even though their limbs were practically torn completely off, they will have full function. The next time we visit Flox, I would like to study their treatments in more depth." Jagman looked at his watch and excused himself. He had some duties to perform.

"Al, what kind of vacation resort do you have in mind for us now?" Fisher asked.

"For some reason I just want to go to the Florida Keys and relax on a nice sun-soaked beach for about 6 days and 5 years," Yates replied.

Fisher and Yates joked about vacation spots as they drank their coffee. Fisher then excused himself as he had duties to perform also. Yates decided to go up to the observation deck to gaze at the stars. He entered the vacant room and sat down to watch the spectrum of star fields and his mind was put to ease. He was just starting to get lost in a deep state of consciousness when he heard what sounded like heavy breathing and passionate kissing. He stood up and abruptly called out,

"ATTENTION ON DECK."

Lieutenant John Marsh and Ensign Barbie King jumped up, both with their shirts unbuttoned.

"Why Lieutenant Marsh and Ensign King, are we enjoying the submarine races? This is no place for officers to be carrying on. What the hell is wrong with you both? Whatever you do on your own time is your business; let's not make it everyone else's. I don't ever want to see OR have anyone else tell me about your love life. If I do hear about it, you both will be put on report. Is that understood?" Yates scolded.

"Yes sir, you won't see or hear about us again" Marsh replied.

"Mr. Marsh, I'm sure they could use some help up in the search center, so why don't you head up there and volunteer your services. That's an order. Ensign King, I'm sure there are some flowers that need tending to, so why don't you tend to them. That too is an order," Yates barked.

The young lovers took heed of the captain's wishes and left immediately. When Marsh and King were out of ear shot the captain shook his head in disbelief and laughed. He then sat back down to enjoy the rest of the star extravaganza. The captain's mind was now rested and clear, and he started back up to the bridge. On his way there he thought he would stop by and check up on what kind of mischief Ensign Washington was getting into. As he was nearing the compartment that housed TRYONE'S PALACE, he heard loud arguing.

"Washington, your machines ripped me off. Hell, I want my money back!" a crewman angrily complained.

The ensign, not wanting to let out the secret that some of his slots may be short changing the players, brought the man out into the passageway to quiet him down.

"Now, here, here, my friend. I run an honest business here. Hell, this place is even sanctioned by Captain Yates himself. And we all know he wouldn't be involved in anything illicit. Now, old Alex and me, we be partners in this here morale building establishment. Hell, that old fucker is so straight they use him as a lubbers line on ships. Now let's talk this over my good friend."

Washington was so confident he was going to dispel the matter smoothly that he put his hand on the bulkhead and leaned into it, lighting up a cigarette and throwing the match down on the deck. He was about to feed the crewman some more jive when he noticed the crewman snap too. He reached behind himself and felt the presence of another person. He slowly felt around the shirt collar and as he feared, felt the insignia of his commanding officer.

"OHHhhh shit, not good," he mumbled.

Washington turned around and stood at attention. He then smiled widely as sweat started to run down his forehead.

"Cappyton, my fine, fine man. How are you today? Sure had a great time on Flox. Well, with your permission sir, I'll get back to tending my business," Washington uttered.

"Stand fast mister. Old fucker am I? You made it sound like I'm in this thing with you. Now what's the problem here?" Yates inquired.

"Nothing sir, just a little malfunction with one of the slots. I was just going to square things up with this fine young lad," Washington answered, gently patting the back of the disgruntled customer.

Captain Yates noticed Father Delaney walking towards them and motioned for him to come over.

"Yes, captain, how may I help you?" the Father asked.

"Sailor, will you excuse us for a moment? Mr. Washington will be with you in a minute or two." The sailor went back inside the Palace. "Father, has Tyrone here met with you in regards to working with you as a morale officer?"

The Priest shook his head no.

"I bet it must have slipped your mind Tyrone, didn't it?" Washington shook his head yes and smiled. "Father, I think the two of you would work well with each other in bolstering the morale of this ship. Perhaps you and Tyrone could incorporate some changes into the Palace. What do you think?"

"Why captain, I think the crew would much enjoy a couple of nice, quiet, fun-filled nights of bingo. Mr. Washington could call out the numbers. I would love working with him," the Father replied.

"Bingo… Bingo…, sheet, can't make no money offa that. Shit, at least I still have the bar," Washington replied.

"OH NO, my son. You have strayed far from the flock. We will serve nice refreshing fruit juices and soft beverages. Put that sinful bar out of your mind," the Father explained.

"Perhaps you two gentlemen need to coordinate your plans. I'll go ahead and close the casino tonight. Don't forget to refund some money, Tyrone."

The captain closed the casino for the evening and left Mr. Washington in the care of Father Delaney. As the captain left for the bridge, he could still hear Ensign Washington complaining about his new business partner.

Yates entered the bridge and conferred with Commander Edwards.

"Ralf, we have to start doing some drills, this crew is getting entirely too lax. We have people making out all over the ship and

Tyrone is starting to short change the crew," Yates complained.

"Ahh, the two love birds Marsh and King. Mr. Marsh said you found them, but didn't go into any detail," Edwards elaborated.

LCDR Hall interrupted. "Sirs, I don't think we have time for a drill, I have a bogie on the screen."

"What's it look like Randy?" Yates asked.

"I not sure, it's still pretty far off. It's big. It could be a ship of some sort," Hall replied.

"What kind of a signature does it have? Is it anything we've run into before?" Edwards inquired.

"Have the boys in the search center lock onto it with the long range scanners," Yates ordered.

Lieutenants Marsh and Williams redirected the ship's radar array towards the incoming ship. It was heading straight for the CONSTELLATION.

Lieutenant Williams informed the Captain, "Sir, she is moving fast on course 1- 6 - 0, straight for us. Her signature isn't in our data banks."

"Commander Edwards, bring CONSTELLATION TO BATTLE STATIONS NOW!" Captain Yates ordered.

Edwards got on the ship's address system and announced, "BATTLE STATIONS, BATTLE STATIONS. THIS IS NOT A DRILL!"

GONG, GONG, GONG, GONG, GONG, the alarms sounded through the ship. The crew stopped their routine duties and ran to their stations.

"All weapons stations reporting armed and ready sir," LCDR Hall announced.

"Reduce speed to one third," Yates ordered the helmsman. "Randy, lock your weapons onto the target."

Both orders were acknowledged by the men. LCDR Lewis called up to the bridge and advised he had two squads of 56's and 1's ready for immediate take off and the balance of his war birds were ready on stand by. Edwards passed the information onto the captain.

Colonel Fisher arrived on the bridge and asked, "Al, what do we have, do you need any assistance from the army?"

"Might not hurt to have some of your men on standby, I'll have Ralf contact Lewis to prepare the shuttles for your troops," Yates responded.

Commander Edwards didn't have to wait for the captains orders. He contacted the air operations office and the two transports were being readied.

"Captain, Captain, those fuckers just took a shot at us!" LCDR Hall yelled.

"Flank speed, evasive maneuvers," Yates ordered.

The helmsman brought Connie's speed up to its maximum, all the while zig-zagging, the ship trying to avoid becoming the receiving end of the projectile fired by the alien craft. Yates ordered LTJG Lister to hail the hostile craft to try and find out why they were attacking. The answer was silence. Then LCDR Hall called back out, "Captain, those bastards just took another pot shot at us."

"Well, I guess they don't want to talk. Hell of a way to welcome folks to the neighborhood," Yates commented.

"Ralf, have Lewis launch his birds, the entire wing. I want half for a CAP over Connie and the rest to attack those bastards on his port flank. Helm, hard to port. Let's see if they want to chase us. If they fall for it, that should set Lewis up for a perfect run at them," Yates ordered.

"Aye sir, turning 0-9-0 degrees, turning hard to port," replied the helm station.

"Randy, permission to fire at will is granted. Indulge yourself," Yates ordered.

LCDR Hall gave all weapons stations the green light to fire. CONSTELLATION let loose her arsenal of laser cannons, laser guns, torpedo's and an assortment of missiles at the alien vessel. The nukes were held back in reserve as a last ditch life saver.

The vessel from an unknown planet fell for the trick, she turned to give chase after the CONSTELLATION, exposing her port side to the ravishes of LCDR Lewis and his fighters. Connie started scoring hits on her aggressor and it slowed their attack. Lewis and his forces came in with an unrelenting punishment, blowing holes in the side of the alien vessel, causing her to break off her attack and turn away.

Yates exclaimed. "O.K. asshole, how do you like them apples. Tag you're it!"

"Turn CONSTELLATION to the right and give pursuit. Ralf, advise the CAP commander that he is free to join in the festivities if the mood strikes them to do so," Yates barked out.

"I roger that captain, I guess we play too rough for them," Edwards replied. The alien space craft was now dead in her tracks. Yates kept his ship at a safe distance, but still well within gun range and CONSTELLATION'S weapons continued hammering its foe, as the F- 56 and ASC-1 fighters repeated their assaults.

"Constellation, Constellation, this is Hawk -1 over. Constellation, Constellation, this is Hawk -1 over," Lewis called over the radio.

"Hawk -1 this is Constellation, go ahead sir."

"Looks like they're trying to launch fighter craft out of the aft end for a counter attack. Over," Lewis continued.

LTJG Lister advised the captain of the alien's intentions. Yates advised her not to let any of their birds get a chance to join in the action. Lister relayed the message to LCDR Lewis.

"Hawk -1, Hawk -1, keep the birds contained, don't let them escape the coop. Over."

"That is a roger. Advise Col. Sanders he'll have some fresh chicken to fry up. Hawk -1 out," Lewis replied.

Lewis massed two squadrons of his fighters at the rear of the alien ship and as it attempted to launch its attack ships, they were destroyed as they left the protection of the mother ship. CONSTELLATION was still hitting the enemy vessel with all of her might and other Hawks and ASC -1's were continuing to make runs on it. The alien captain was ready to give up the fight. He was quite aware that his adversary had outfoxed him in tactics. After the beating at Connie's last port of call, this victory greatly bolstered her crew's morale.

"Captain, I'm getting a signal from the enemy ship. I'm running it through the translator. I'll put it on the speaker sir," Lister conveyed.

"I am called Yalt, I am the commander of the Battle Cruiser ZILOD. I wish hostilities to cease. My weapons will be turned off," came a voice over the bridge speakers.

ZILOD stopped firing her weapons. Captain Yates ordered his forces to cease fire, but stand ready. The battle was now at a lull.

With a cease fire in place, it was agreed that the two ship commanders would meet. A shuttle craft from CONSTELLATION was dispatched over to the ZILOD and returned with the captain. Yates,

Fisher and Edwards waited for Yalt in the air operations debriefing room.

An armed security detail escorted Yalt into the room, they then stood guard just outside the door. Yates invited his adversary to sit as he made introductions, then asked,

"Why did you fire on my ship?"

The alien captain stated, "My planet in is ruins and my people are dying. Strangers from foreign worlds, who have posed as being peaceful and friendly have shown us nothing but deceit. They have exploited our resources and contaminated our home, leaving our people starving and diseased. The ruling council of Zelcor has ordered its remaining military forces to dissuade any likely aggressors from destroying our world any further."

Commander Edwards asked, "So you shoot first and ask questions later?"

"I do not understand your question," Yalt said.

Yates stepped in and explained what the commander meant, then stated,

"We are travelers lost in the universe. We mean no harm to anyone. If we are challenged we will fight, and we fight to win. We did try to communicate with you by radio, the only reply we got from you was a missile heading down our throats."

Yalt paused for moment before giving his reply. "We have been tricked many times before. Our world can no longer take that chance. I do believe you are not of a treacherous nature. You have not destroyed my ship, instead you wished to talk."

Col Fisher entered the conversation. "As Captain Yates has said, we do come in peace, but we will defend ourselves. We do understand your people's plight. We have helped others who have been oppressed. Perhaps we can assist your world."

Yalt, looking confused, replied, "We have waged battle against you and you want to help us?"

"Yes, if you will permit us. Maybe our science departments can find a way to reverse your misfortunes. We may be able to prove to your ruling council that not all foreigners have evil intentions. We can start building a trust right here and now, if not we shall resume our travels."

"Captain, your people seem honorable. Let us build. My ship is badly damaged and many of my crew have been injured. It will take some time before I can lead you to my home planet," Yalt replied.

"If you will permit, we will send some of our technicians and medical staff to your ship to help with repairs and give aid to your injured. You will have to guarantee their safety," Yates responded.

After further discussions, arrangements were made to send crew members from CONSTELLATION over to the ZILOD to help with repairs and to tend to the injured. Some of the more critical cases would be treated aboard Connie. Several medical personnel from the ZILOD were brought back to Connie as consultants of the Zelcor physiology.

CONSTELLATION secured from battle stations and the majority of fighter craft were ordered back to the hanger deck, leaving only a small C.A.P. in service in case of trouble.

Ensign Washington was among the first to arrive on board ZILOD. He looked around at the overwhelming wreckage of the crippled ship, and all he could do was mutter to himself,

"Shit, I'm gonna need a whole bunch of Elmer's Glue to fix this mutha fucker. I hope they brought over all them translator boxes, I can't understand a word these crackers are saying. Muthas must be from Jersey."

"Pardon me, Mr. Washington, I didn't catch all of that," came a voice from behind. It was Commander Edwards.

"Yo, lil boss, what's this shit? We find somebody whose asses we can kick after they start shootin' at us, then we be sleeping with them? Shit, you got this brother confused," Washington asked.

"Tyrone, think of it this way. We help these people out, we get invited back to their planet, they feel indebted to us. You can open up a casino and I bet they will flock to it," Edwards replied.

"I see what you're saying brother. Hell, yes. We be the U.N., only with a payback. I see all kinds of business opportunities here. Ralf, you're the man with the plan. And it's gonna be money in our hand," Washington greedily shot out rubbing his hands in expectation.

The commander put his arm around Washington and said,

"Tyrone, my good friend, my name is COMMANDER EDWARDS. Now let's get some work done here mister, NOW!"

Washington snapped out of his dream world and led his work crew into the task of getting the ZILOD functional. After several days of hard work, the mission started to show signs of success. Trust was being developed, and the once adversaries were now showing signs of reliance on each other.

Repairs on ZILOD were completed as best as could be done in space. The two ships turned to a course that would bring them to the planet Zelcor. Travel was slow, and it gave the two races the time and opportunity to learn about each other's worlds. The fear of being fooled into deception soon faded.

Captain Yates and Yalt, along with members of CONSTELLATION science departments held conferences on the extent of environmental, biological and medical problems faced by the people of Zelcor.

A plan for testing the atmosphere and soil would be headed up by LCDR Wang and Ensign King. Medical issues would be headed up by Commander Jagman. Infrastructure would be a joint team effort commanded by LCDR Malloy with assistance from Lieutenants Marsh and Williams and Ensign Washington.

By the end of the sixth day of travel, the planet Zelcor loomed on the horizon. The planet's atmosphere appeared to have a bright green tint and its bodies of water peered through with a yellow color. The land masses were light brown, with spotty patches of green. According to Yalt, this was the aftermath of years of decay and the rape of the planet's natural resources by predators from foreign worlds who came with false friendships. Yalt indicated that his world once resembled that of earth, as he viewed photographic images shown to him by the CONSTELLATION command.

The Zelcor ruling council granted permission for CONSTELLATION to land, along with ZILOD at the military space port on the outskirts of its capitol city called Raznard.

CHAPTER 5

# ZELCOR THE FADING WORLD

After the two ships were secured from landing Yalt had arranged for a meeting of the Zelcor Ruling council and the earth commanders. Due to the poor modes of transportation Col Fisher had his men prepared several hummers for the trip. One vehicle would carry Yates, Fisher and Yalt, while the other two would be security escorts, one in front and the other behind the command vehicle.

As they traveled through the city, they took noticed the condition of their surroundings. The metropolis at one time must have been a show case of art, science and culture that would have surpassed any intelligent civilization the earthlings have seen thus far. Now the decaying capital resembled an urban slum.

The buildings were falling apart, rubble lay everywhere in the streets. People were huddled in small groups, dressed in rags and the odor of their filth drifted across the area on a soft breeze. Inhabitants could be seen hunting as a food source a small rodent-like animal that were eating the rotting corpses littering the conurbation. Yates and Fisher were appalled by the sights and occasionally glanced over at Yalt, who rode with his head held high.

The small convoy arrived at its destination, the chambers of the ruling council, and entered the meeting place. Yalt introduced his new-found friends to his superiors. Yates brought along one of the translator devices to help ease the communication barrier, until the council grasped a working knowledge of the English language.

Captain Yates and Colonel Fisher explained how the two peoples had met in battle. They went on to say that it was the way of the people of earth to help others in need. Yalt supported any plan that might aid his people and he helped convince the Ruling Council that the intentions of the earth space travelers were not to trick or exploit the people of Zelcor. The council left the chamber to decide in private if they would accept the help offered. They returned within a short period of time and announced that the help Yates and Fisher proposed would be welcomed.

Yates and Fisher went back to the ship and called a meeting of the three specialized groups in the forward deck 6 conference room.

Yates opened the meeting with a brief summary about the sad state of affairs of the civilization.

"To put it point blank, things are a mess here. I don't know if we can do anything to help. Perhaps if we would have arrived here ten years ago, it would have been a different scenario. The city is on the verge of complete collapse, and from what we have learned today from the ruling council, every town on the planet is in the same shape. Most of the people here are undernourished and sick or dying. The atmosphere, soil, and water supply for the most part have been completely contaminated from war, exploitation of natural resources, and heavy chemical pollution. It's not a pretty sight here. There is a lot of work to do, and with any luck we can help make a difference. We can only do what we can do, but we will give it our best shot. Yalt has prepared packets. They are in front of you. These packets detail the worse of the worse that you will be dealing with in your fields of expertise. He and others from Zelcor will be meeting with your teams shortly. The translation between our language and theirs is at times difficult, so the person to person aspect will be of great help. Also LTJG Lister has translator boxes in each of the meeting rooms. That's all I have to say, except good luck. Sam, do you have anything?"

"Yes, I do. Thank you captain. My career in the United States Army spans quite a few years. I have never seen a civilization in as bad of shape as this one. Yalt even confessed to us that the battle cruiser ZILOD was manned with only half of its complement. The rest of the crew were too sick to be deployed. The Zelcor people have a lot of pride, but they know when they need help, and they need it now. I have offered my command to Captain Yates for any duty that may be required. Captain Webb and LT Atkins will be your contact, just get a hold of them and you will get the support requested. That's it for me, GOOD LUCK," Fisher stated.

The teams were dismissed and they went to their assigned meeting rooms to work with their Zelcor counterparts to map out a strategic plan for reconstruction that would begin the next day.

The meetings ended and each team was upbeat in hopes they could play a part in saving the planet, and an entire civilization. Webb and Atkins were already being hit up for requests for transportation for the following day. They were assured that all appeals would be met.

As the early dawn broke, two small convoys left CONSTELLATION. One headed into the city and consisted of the medical and infrastructure teams, dubbed by the crew the "support team". The other group headed out into the country. It contained the atmospheric/soil team and would be called the "ecology team".

As the support team entered the city they were awestruck, the same as Yates and Fisher were the day before. They could not believe the desolation and destruction.

Washington was muttering as he observed the eyesore. "Sheet, this worse than the hood in Newark on a bad day. I can't believe these dudes are still alive."

Everyone in the vehicle agreed with his comment. The support team's plan was twofold - first it wanted to inspect the medical facilities to get them up and running, then inspect the power plant. If need be they could rig up generators at the river to produce the needed power. It was hoped that by supplying power to the hospital, the sick and injured could be treated, and once recovered they too would be able to help with the rebuilding.

The ecology team's mission for the day was to take air, soil and water samples at different locations and then to identify the toxins and try to come up with compounds that would neutralize the contaminants. As they took their samples they were in amazement at the soil. In most places it was dry and barren, with a substance hard as concrete on top, then the brown gradually changed into a red and yellow crusty material covering miles of the planet's surface. The rivers contained a pollutant that made the water run yellow, and it also affected the planet's oceans, turning them the same color of the putrid feeders. Air samples also contained a number of pollutants. If vegetation could be restored to this dying world it would help filter out the elements.

Before returning to the ship they took soil samples from beneath a small patch of foliage they spotted on a nearby hill. They would compare the chemical makeup of this specimen against the areas that supported no growth at all. Upon their arrival back at the science lab

Letam, one of the ZelcORION scientists was waiting for them. As Ensign King was preparing the soil samples for testing, LCDR Wang quizzed him.

"Letam, exactly when did the vegetation start to die off on the planet?"

"It started to happen years ago after a war with an invader from a far-off world. First they attacked using a very destructive weapon that left high levels of radiation across large areas of the planet's surface. As our people were forced to retreat away from the area, they started to mine an element called zotar. The ore is very valuable, once refined it can be used as fuel for space craft, and it can be used as a powerful weapon as well. They were careless the way they retrieved the ore from the ground. The method used would be comparable to the outlawed strip mining done on your home planet. We were finally able to ward off these aggressors. As the abundance of this ore soon spread through the galaxy, others who pretended to be our friends repeated this same travesty over and over again. One of the intruders sprayed the surface with deadly chemicals, causing a great amount of lives to be lost and the destruction of our forest. Soon our planet became what you see now," Letam responded.

LCDR Wang then said, "I see you have been studying our history. These bombs you refer to sound very much like our nuclear weapons. A very dirty and powerful destructive device. We have a lot of work ahead of us. However, I don't think all is lost. I see hope. Some vegetation was able to survive, this is where we will build from!"

"LCDR Wang, the chemical makeup of the uncontaminated soil is very much like that of earths. I would like to transplant some of our vegetable seedlings to see if they will grow in the outside environment," King interrupted.

Wang agreed. As she called down for transportation, King went and obtained the tiny plants from the hydroponics unit of the ship.

The three of them went back to one of the surviving foliage plots and planted the seedlings.

The support team was busy checking out their assigned areas. The medical facility, as run down as it was, had very a competent staff, although they lacked power and medical supplies. Marsh and Washington checked out the circuitry of the building. It looked like it could be operational with a little coaxing. Officials from the ruling council brought over blue prints of the city's electrical grid. They traced the routing back to the power production plant and that is where they found problems.

They found the equipment inside the plant in shambles; generators were burnt out, parts were broken or missing from machinery, and there was serious oxidation of metal parts.

"Maybe at one time these folks would have been considered centuries ahead of us, but their power system isn't much different than ours. I just bet we can rebuild this thing," Marsh stated."

"What, you mean we can rebuild this thing. YOU MEAN old Tyrone gonna be rebuilding this thing? You mutha fucking cracker SIR, you'll bet on this shit, but you won't bet on my slots," Washington snapped.

Marsh came back with, "I have a better chance in winning here. Hell, your slots haven't a chance of being fixed, or should I say they are FIXED? By the way Tyrone, how do you spell slots - B-I-N-G-O."

"Fuck you sir, let's get back to work. I'll get my boyz in here and take the good parts from the decent machine and make copies of them on the duplicators. I know we will have this place up and running, so then I can have some funning, after I gets done with the dubbin," Washington sang out.

The work crews took the one machine that was in good shape

apart, carefully cataloging where each piece came from. There was a steady stream of traffic going to and from the ship, replicating each part and then returning them. The pace kept up all through the night. By mid morning the next day the 'good' generator was put back together, then the second, all down the line until all the units in this plant were repaired. A solar array was added as a booster to the system and to also act as a backup power source. Now it was time to power up. To insure fires didn't break out all over the city from electrical shorts, all the grids were switched off, except the one that the medical facility was left on. LCDR Malloy arrived at the plant to give the order to turn the power on.

"What you doing here?" Washington asked Malloy.

"Well Tyrone, I'm here to make sure things got done correctly. Hell, the way you rigged your slots, I'm quite worried about whether you have this thing fucked up or not,"

Malloy replied.

"Shit, you just here to take all the credit ain't you? Sheet, my slots are good. I built them myself," Washington rebuffed.

"Oh, I know, poor, poor little Tyrone. Oh, by the way Mr. Washington, I walked by your little tourist trap the other day and I noticed that your sign was misspelled. It should have been spelled B-I-N-G-O instead of P-A-L-A-C-E," Malloy joked.

Washington walked off flustered, talking to himself. Malloy turned his attention to the machinery, checking to make sure everything was ready for the power up. All systems were a go and the order was given. The solar panels were opened to the sun. Nothing happened. All the switches and relays were double-checked, but nothing was found to be wrong. Then suddenly Washington yelled.

"Who the hell forgot to connect the solar array to the generators? Sheet, you want something done right, you have to do it yourself. As usual, never fear Tyrone is here, quit scratching your hair, and pass me a beer, and get me a chair."

Washington corrected the oversight and soon lights on the generators went from a dim glow to shiny bright. The machinery started to hum as it went on line.

Malloy radioed Jagman at the medical facility and reported the good news - the facility had power. For the first time in years the medical staff had something to smile about. They had power, and the badly needed medicines were being produced aboard CONSTELLATION, in turn to re-supply the hospital. Soon the death toll would decrease, as well as the depressing frustration of the Zelcor medical staff.

The support staff called it a day, and as they headed back to ship for the daily debriefing, they noticed the army contingent of CONSTELLATION'S crew busy making repairs to the structures of the city. Colonel Fisher had ordered blades put back on the front of his tanks so they could be used as bulldozers. The iron war horses were now being used to fight another kind of war - a war to save lives. The machines were plowing through the vast amount of rubble, depositing it into mounds for later removal from the city. The cleanup and salvation of the Zelcor people was now in full swing.

The debriefing started promptly at 1800 hours Yates, Edwards and Fisher also attended.

"O. K., what's the lowdown for the day?" Yates asked.

"Commander Jagman gave his report. "Captain, the medical facility is operational. Literally it is. Surgery is being performed as we speak. Medical supplies are still low, but they are increasing. We plan on visiting one of the outer-lying hospitals tomorrow to see what we can do for it. We had a good day today. Lives were saved. End of report, sir."

"That's great news, Dave. Thank you. Father Delaney has offered his services to you in any way he can help, you may want to contact him," Yates replied.

"He is more than welcome. I'll get with him after chow," Jagman answered back.

"Next, Lieutenant Commander Malloy, let's hear from you"" Yates requested.

"Captain, As Dr. Jagman stated, we had a good day. It took us all night, but the main power plant is up and running. Tomorrow we plan on looking at some of the sub-stations to see what we can do with them. The crews worked hard, it wasn't easy, we practically had to rebuild everything from scratch. One final note, I am quite confident that Ensign Washington can now spell bingo," Malloy stated.

The attendees all burst out with laughter as Washington slouched down in his chair. Lieutenant Williams started to sing "B-i-n-g-o, b-i-n-g-o, b-i-n-g-o, bingo was his game-o." After the brief lull, Yates continued with the meeting.

"Lieutenant Commander Wang, what did your investigations turn up?" Yates asked.

Wang responded, "Captain, we are quite flustered. We have been working with Letam, one of the scientists assigned to us by the Zelcor Ruling Council. He explained to Ensign King and I about how the contaminations occurred over the years of war and environmental carelessness. We are trying to analyze the different compounds in the good and bad soils and water samples to try and come up with a neutralizing agent. But so far we have batted zero. Ensign King is finishing up on a water test. She should be here shortly."

Just as Wang finished her report, King entered the room and she had a smile on her face.

Yates greeted her with, "Ensign King, glad you could join us. Is that smile good news or did you run into Lieutenant Marsh?"

The now blushing petite blond ensign took a seat and replied, "Oh, captain."

She then opened a folder and gave her report.

"I think we have a breakthrough. I have been working on a water sample we took from the river by the water holding place. You know, were the water goes into that water treatment thing. Anyway, I tried using all the neutralizing agents I could think of, nothing worked. I just wanted to cry. I was so angry that I slapped my hand on the counter. You know what? I broke a nail."

The attendees were now looking up at the ceiling, some were tapping their pencils and others twirling their thumbs. She continued. "As I reached to look at my pinky, I accidentally spilled the container of that yucky water into a pan of water lilies that I was going to take down to deck 5 later on. I said a bad word when that happened. But you know what? The yellow water started to fade and soon it became clear. I ran some tests on it and it was pure."

Yates shook his head and boomed, "WHAT?"

King re-iterated. "The water lilies purified the nasty water. Maybe we should try and take some outside. I know where there is a small pond we could try it on."

Commander Edwards joined in. "My god, if we can clean up the water, that's half the battle. How many water lilies do we have ensign?"

King replied in a serious juvenile way. "We have lots, but I don't think enough to put around the entire planet, commander."

"Ensign King, I bet you are correct, we don't have enough for the entire planet, but we have enough to start the process. Al, I say we go for it, let's see if the pond clears up, then we can move them around. The plants will multiply, so in time there will be enough," Commander Edwards stated.

"Ralf, I agree, let's get them out there. Ensign King, take some to the pond in the morning. One other thing Ralf, don't use the word 'BET' in front of Mr. Washington. You know how sensitive he is about that," the captain quipped.

The room once again echoed with laughter as Ensign Washington slouched further down in his chair.

"Sam, what does the army have for us?" Yates asked.

"Well, we got a lot of rubble cleared up today. Raznard is almost in as good a condition as Berlin was in 1945. There is a hell of a lot more to do. We saw what looked to be bomb craters on the outskirts of the city and we're filling them in with the debris. If Miss King here does have a way to clean up the water, maybe we should start working on getting the water plant up to full power. That's all I have for you, Al," Fisher responded.

LCDR Wang poised a question to Fisher and the captain. "Sirs, the water is contaminated with chemical runoff from the rain. The crust on top of the soil is very hard indeed. I propose we conduct a second experiment in the morning. Ensign King has made reference to 'A' pond, in fact there are two ponds side by side. Why don't we put water lilies in both of them and if they clear up, bulldoze the crusty layer of toxic waste into one of the ponds to see if the lilies would neutralize it. We would also be exposing the soil to the atmosphere, and with any luck it may in time become fertile again."

Yates agreed with the idea. Power and water was a good start, but food would be needed to be grown to feed the starving citizens of this society. Nourishment was barely being provided on what little uncontaminated land there was. Meat was very scarce due to the lack of grazing space. If the second experiment succeeded, this too would change. A to-do list for the following day was drafted and the meeting was brought to a close.

Yates, Fisher and Edwards remained seated in the conference room and Yates asked, "Who's standing watch?"

Edwards replied. "Hall is right now.  Lewis will relieve him at 2400 hrs."

"Well, gentlemen, that gives us some time to kill. Anyone up for experimentation on the intoxicating effects some fine Irish whiskey can produce?  If so, let us adjourn to my cabin," Yates invited.

The three men left the room and proceeded down to the captain's quarters. Edwards and Fisher plopped down in chairs and Fisher rested his feet on the desk. Yates opened a bottle of Jamison's and poured each of them a drink. Commander Edwards shook his head and started to laugh.

"What's so funny?" Yates asked.

The commander replied. "King, she is good at her job and cute as the dickens, but sometimes I can't help feeling she is five blades short of a six bladed propeller."

Fisher commented, "She is a cutie by all means, but she has a lot of growing to do. I hope Marsh knows how lucky he is tapping into that."

"Al, she kind of reminds me of that navy nurse you met in Honolulu when you got hurt on the NIMITZ a few years back," Edwards teasingly remarked.

"Ralf, let's not get into that, it's a story we need to forget about." Yates replied.

"Alright, does the CONSTELLATION'S Captain have some bones

is his closet? Tell me about it Al. Pour me a fresh one before you start," Fisher queried.

"Sam, it was a long time ago. I had just gotten engaged to my wife. NIMITZ was on a training cruise, I was landing my F-14 Tomcat when the hook broke. I managed to put myself and the plane into the drink. I must have banged my head pretty bad, when I woke up there was the sweetest looking angel peering down at me. She asked me how I felt."

Commander Edwards started laughing uncontrollably and exclaimed, "Sam, this is the good part, you're going to love this."

The captain continued his story with a smirk on his face.

"Well, I told her it hurts right down there, long story short it was the best convalescing of my life."

"Sounds to me it was more of a molesting than a convalescing," Fisher joked.

"The best part of it is, the nurse was an admiral's daughter, who just happened to be Al's C.O.'s brother. Shortly after that Al was transferred over to the Atlantic Fleet," Edwards interjected.

The three men stayed up and chatted about past conquests, killing off the entire bottle and enjoying every minute of it.

A new day was born and the ecology team was the first to leave the ship. LCDR Wang, Ensign King and Letam were driven to the ponds. The convoy consisted of two hummers, the first transporting the team and the second hauling the water lilies that were going to be used in the experiment. Upon arrival King grabbed her testing kits, assisted by Letam, and took water samples from each of the ponds. LCDR Wang was being helped by the army drivers in bringing the tubs containing water lilies down to the ponds.

With the water samples taken and logged in, the five team members proceeded to place equal amounts of the plants into each pool of water.

Letam looked to his earth counterparts and said, "This experiment may not have the same results as those in your lab. The toxins are of higher concentration and in an uncontrolled environment. Please do not be discouraged if it fails. We have been trying to fix this problem for a long time."

LCDR Wang replied. "Letam, we can prepare for the worst and pray for the best. We will not let the frustration of failure deter our mission's goal in any way."

"Heck Letam, everything will be alright. LT Marsh told me it would and I believe him. Oh dang it, I broke another nail," King affirmed.

Letam, looking confused over King's comment looked to LCDR Wang, who was smiling. She told Letam she would explain later. The team packed up their gear and headed back to the ship. They would return the following day to see if there was any change in the water quality.

As the ecology team returned to the ship, the support team was just starting to make their trip into the City of Raznard. Once inside the city the team would divide up into two groups. Jagman and Delaney would go and check out the other smaller medical facilities and Malloy and his crew would check on the electrical sub-stations. Col Fisher had asked Captain Webb to take a group of soldiers the night before to start work on the water treatment plant and they were already hard at work.

This was the first trip into the city for Father Delaney, the man was fighting hard to hold back tears as he watched the desperate people trying to cling to life. He had to turn his head away as he saw children trying to walk, but they were so weak their legs bent underneath them; others were cutting up dead bodies for food.

"This has to be the cruelest sight I ever have witnessed. These beings have been reduced to savages. May the Lord pity them and have mercy on their souls," he confided to his friend, Dr. Jagman.

"Thomas, I understand completely your dismay. There is one redeeming factor that you have to take into consideration. These people have not yet lost their will to survive. With food at the level it is, they must resort to these primitive survival instincts. If we can get their ecological system working again, this will come to a stop. We then can pray for them, they will be forgiven. They are using the dead for life sustaining purposes, not creating death," Jagman counseled.

The remainder of the support team found their target, one of the substations.

They exited their vehicle and went inside for a look.

"Sheet, this mother fucker is empty, better call the poeleece to apprehend those villains," Washington called out.

"They cannibalized this one for parts to keep the others going. Let's find the next one and see what it needs, then we can duplicate parts and rebuild this one," the LCDR conveyed.

They secured the building and checked the map for the next location. They had to take detours because of collapsed buildings blocking the roadway. Finally, they reached the second sub-station and went inside.

"Now this is a little more like it," LT Williams said.

The interior and equipment were intact. In fact it looked like it had never been used.

"Washington, bring me the electrical stations map plan," Malloy ordered.

Tyrone brought over a piece of paper and handed it to him. As the lieutenant commander glanced down to study the document he yelled out, "Washington, what the hell is this?"

Washington went back over to Malloy to see what he was complaining about and took a look at the sheet of paper.

"Sorry about that, I thought the last place would make a nice casino. I was just drawing up some plans for it. Hee, hee, here is the sheet you need. I'll just take these," Washington softly said.

With one near new power sub-station in their hands, repairing the remainder would be a cake walk. The rest of the stations were toured that day and a scheduled plan for bringing each station back on line was drawn up. Soon the entire city would have power. Then power would be produced for the remaining cities. As darkness was drawing near, a trail of tail lights could be seen heading back to the star cruiser. For one team, it had been a second day of positive results. The daily debriefing took place and, as usual, the plan for the next days work objectives was drawn up. The command passed along to the crew a message of thanks and hope that had been conveyed to Captain Yates from the Zelcor Ruling Council when he met with them earlier that day.

Once again morning came and the ecology team headed out to the ponds to see if the experiment had worked. Captain Yates went along. Ensign King seemed a little jittery on the ride. She had concerns the toxin may have been too strong for the plants to handle.

The two vehicles arrived. King jumped out first and ran toward the ponds. The rest of the team, who were further back heard a scream. They hurried their pace to see what was the matter. They observed King jump up and run to the other pond, then they heard her yelling "YES, YES, YES".

LCDR Wang looked at the captain and said, "Captain, is LT Marsh

here, I don't recall inviting him."

"I don't know Laura, but something indeed has her excited," Yates replied.

"Captain, LCDR Wang, look, look, the water is clear. It worked," King yelled.

She was so excited that she was dropping her sample tubes, she tried picking them back up, but they kept falling from her hands. LCDR Wang and Yates caught up with her, Wang bent down to take the samples for her.

"Ensign King, congratulations. Can you test these samples here in the field or do we have to go back to the ship?" Yates asked.

"Thank you captain, I have the data sheets with me and I brought a portable test thing with me, I can't think of the name of it now, I'll perform the analysis right away. I wish John was here," replied King.

The tests were completed and King announced the water tested pure. A third hummer pulled up with Colonel Fisher and Letam. He had arrived late at the ship and Fisher brought him out. The two men walked down to the pond to join the rest of the team.

"Well, from the looks on your faces, it seems we have good news," Fisher assumed.

"Yes we do. Ensign King, why don't you tell the Colonel and Letam what it is," LCDR Wang joyfully replied.

"It worked, that old dirty water is clean and clear. Letam, I told you not to worry," King replied.

Fisher got on his radio and ordered one of his tank's that was fitted out with a blade to come up to their location. When the tank arrived, the tank commander was ordered to scrape the yellow chemical crust off of the soil and into one of the ponds. The tank made several runs and the crusty substance was pushed into the water and colored it the murky yellow. King took new samples.

Letam was elated by the success of the experiment. His planet now had hope of surviving.

"Captain, years ago we saw this tragedy unfolding in front of our eyes. We have a facility at our ice cap that contains hundreds of frozen embryos of each life form and flora that inhabited our planet. We did this in hopes that one day the contamination would reverse itself. That day has come. Life will be as it was in the past on my planet. Thank you and your crew for our salvation," Letam expressed.

"We still have a lot of work ahead of us, this is only a drop in the bucket," Yates replied.

While they were talking, King was busy moving some of the water lilies from the clean pond over to the contaminated one. She started to take new samples for testing. The test showed levels of contamination were already starting to decrease. She shared her findings with the others. The major question then, how could the surface of the entire planet be uncontaminated? Pushing the pollutants into ponds and rivers would fill them up, there had to be another source of cleansing. Additional samples of the yellow crust were gathered and brought back to the ship and a massive battery of tests were begun.

It was late night and the research teams needed a break. They had come up with nothing. They gathered in the officer's mess for coffee and frustration filled the room. Tyrone Washington entered and noticed how depressed the mood was and he decided to try and cheer them up.

"WAZZUP, WAZZUP, why all the gloomy faces? Shit, The Four Topps had a song about this - 'A ROOM OF GLOOM'. Shit, this looks more like the room of doom. Why all the sad faces?" he asked.

"Washington, has anybody told you, you have the worst timing?

To answer your question, we can't find a way to decontaminate the soil," LCDR Wang replied.

"HHHmmm, I see. Sheet, I gots an idea, why don't we build some lil ol water carts, dig little holes in the nasty yellow stuff, fill them with water and drop in a lily pad?" Washington said.

Wang snapped to her feet and started to scold him. "Mr. Washington, that has got to be the most stu.... No, wait a minute - it will be an enormous undertaking, but it may work. By god, that just may do the trick. It's our only choice. You're a genius."

She went over to him and kissed him on the cheek and then went to find the captain. Washington stood there for a moment grinning ear to ear and then jokingly said,

"It must be love, she wants me. Did you see that? Oh, boy I'm having takeout tonight."

He was invited to join the remaining team members, the mood now one of jubilation. Wang caught up with the captain on the bridge. She told him of Washington's idea and the great possibility that it might work. Yates called Fisher and told him of the idea. Fisher advised he would have some of his men build some portable water wagons. He had done this kind of thing during the Gulf War. The tanks could draw water from inside the city. The next day pot holes were drilled in the crusty substance, filled with water and a lily pad plant. The work was slow and tedious. The results were slow, but it was working. As larger plots of soil were exposed, grass and shrubs were planted and the greenery started replacing the yellow-coated, brown barren soil. As more and more foliage took root, Mother Nature herself was able to start to slowly reverse the damage caused by the treacherous aggressors of the past. LCDR Lewis and Zelcor science teams visited the embryo storage facility at the icecap and retrieved the frozen offspring, bringing them back to Raznard in the transports. The simplest life forms were the first to be re-introduced into the ecology system, and as they multiplied the next higher level of life was brought back into the system.

Within weeks wildlife and foliage was becoming the norm instead of the exception. The people of Zelcor were now able to fend for themselves as they became stronger. The cities across the planet started to spring back to life one by one, and the civilization's basic pride returned. Food stockpiles, however still low, were easing as each day went by. The people of Zelcore were in debt to CONSTELLATION'S crew, and very grateful.

CHAPTER 6

# THE ANTORIC EXPERIENCE

With the crises on Zelcor coming to its conclusion the CONSTELLATION was getting ready to head back into space to continue the quest of finding her way home.

The Zelcor Ruling Council paid a surprise visit to the star cruiser shortly before she was ready to leave. They gave their final thanks to the captain and crew for their efforts in bringing the dying planet back to life. The commanding officer of the ZILOD was assigned the honor of escorting CONSTELLATION to the outer reaches of their system.

The last of the hatches were secured on the cruiser and the report to Captain Yates was given.

"Captain, all departments report ready, we can taxi on your order," Edwards relayed.

"Very well, you know the routine Ralf, let's get underway," Yates ordered.

CONSTELLATION started her approach for take off and the ZILOD was right behind her. Both ships took off within seconds of each other and headed into space leaving a grateful world behind them. It took several days to reach the outer edge of the system when a message came from their escort.

"Captain, I have a message from the ZILOD," LTJG Lister reported.

"Patch it through to the ships P.A. system," Yates ordered.

"Yalt, this is Yates, go ahead with your transmission," Yates transmitted.

"To our friends of earth, a sincere thanks from our people. It is the wishes of our planet's inhabitants that you finally find your way home. We hope one day to rejoin with you. That day will be a great celebration. The crew of the Zelcor Battle Cruiser ZILOD wish you latermoustric. It means have a safe voyage."

The radio transmission ended and the ZILOD veered off course to starboard for her return journey home. The captain and the bridge crew watched the ZILOD disappear into space on the main monitor. Yates thought to himself, how ironic it was, the two peoples met in hard battle, and now it was hard to leave as new friends.

CONSTELLATION continued on her course away from ZELCOR, again charting new ground, at least as far as the earthlings were concerned.

"Mr. Hall, take the com. LTJG Lister have Colonel Fisher meet me in the officers mess. Ralf, care to join us?" Yates called.

Yates and Edwards went to the mess and grabbed some coffee then found a table. Fisher came in shortly afterwards and joined them. The three men exchanged pleasantries. Then Yates got down to business.

"Before we left Zelcor I had a chat with Yalt. He advised me we would be passing through the Antoric System. He strongly urged the use of caution while in the influence of it. He didn't go into great detail, the last ZelcORION ship to pass through it was over a hundred years ago," Yates explained.

"What happened?" Fisher questioned.

Yates went on to explain further. "He didn't really have an answer. The ship named the NOVAED came back on auto pilot. There wasn't a soul on board. The ship's logs last entry advised they were attacked by an unknown vessel. It isn't clear if they were boarded of if they abandoned ship due to battle damage. She was torn up pretty bad."

"Al, is there any way we can skirt around the system?" Edwards asked.

"According to Yalt the system contains 18 planets and covers a humongous area of space. The system is bordered on one side by a heavy radiation belt. He doubted whether our ship could withstand passing through it. So we have no choice but to cut through the system," Yates continued.

"Does he expect we will run into trouble?" Fisher asked

"Hell it's been over a hundred years since their last ship entered it. It may not even have been the inhabitants of the system who attacked the NOVAED," Edwards commented.

"That's true Ralf, he just wanted us to know of possible danger. If we all stay on our toes, we should be alright," Yates said.

I'll have my boys keep an extra eye out for anything unusual, and

I'll have Webb get with LCDR Hall, maybe we can double up on the ship's security patrols," Fisher added.

"This morning I briefly mentioned to Hall to keep his eyes open for anything funny. Ralf, if you would fill him in on things and make sure he meets with Captain Webb," Yates concluded.

The short meeting ended. Yates and Edwards parted company with Fisher and both men returned to the bridge.

CONSTELLATION continued on her journey and was drawing closer to the Antoric System. LT's Marsh and Williams were busy in the search center scanning the space around them when Williams saw a gigantic blip on his screen.

"Holy shit John, look at this," Williams yelled.

Marsh went over to take a look. He had never seen an image on the screen that big before. "We better tell the captain," he told Williams.

"Captain, we have a contact Bering 3-5-5 degrees off the port bow. It's a big son of a bitch, its got to be at least ten million miles long," he yelled.

Yates then ordered, "Turn on the cameras and put it on the main screen."

The main viewing screen on the bridge lit up, showing the contact. All eyes were glued to the screen, which showed a multi-colored gaseous cloud that stretched as far as they could see. The hazy image was that of a rainbow of colored lights - yellows, reds, and greens, which emitted skyrocketing sparkles of various colors and saturations.

Commander Edwards could not take his eyes off of it and in a very low voice said, "It's a nebula, it's a damn nebula. Look at how awesome it is."

"This must be the radiation belt Yalt was speaking of. Helm, come right 5-0 degrees to new heading 0-4-5. We need to stay clear of that thing," Yates ordered.

The helmsman heeded to the captain's request and turned the ship to her new course, giving them some breathing room from the nebula. The news of this fantastic sight spread around the ship in no time at all. All the monitors in the ship were crowded by crew members watching the spectacle. The ship experienced slight vibrations caused by the different types of radiation intermixing with each other and then exploding, sending its shock waves out into space. The silence on the bridge due to this magnificent spectrum of light and color was broken by the words of LT Marsh.

"Skipper, we must be entering the Antoric System. I'm picking up additional contacts on my screen. They appear to be reflections of planets," he stated.

"Helm, reduce speed to one quarter," the captain ordered.

The ship reduced her speed and slowly entered the star system. Commander Edwards ordered the scanner and radar systems be put on maximum search so nothing could sneak up on CONSTELLATION and surprise her. The Air Ops department was put on standby alert for precautionary measures due to the words of warning from Yalt. Connie was expecting the unexpected and was prepared for it. The ship's commanders learned from the lessons of this journey not to leave anything to chance again.

As CONSTELLATION entered the star system the Search Center crew was plotting the orbital paths of its 18 planets. Commander Edwards checked in with them and inquired about the status of their work. Williams advised him that they had completed the assignment and the plots were printing out now. Edwards was handed the report and he took it to the captain and said,

"Al, the boys have finished mapping out the orbital paths of the planets. Care to take a look?"

The two men studied the chart and Yates commented.

"Looks like Antoric 17 and 18 may be well behind us. Their paths go right smack into the nebula. I doubt very much if there would be any life on those planets."

"I agree with you Al, according to this it looks like planet 16 is in front of us a little off to starboard. Since we're only about six months late for dinner back home, I don't suppose another year or two will not make that much difference. Let's say we check it out," Edwards cited.

The captain grinned and shook his head in agreement and he ordered the ship be turned and head for Antoric 16. The ship traveled for several days and finally reached the planet. The ship was maneuvered into an orbit around the sphere. LCDR Lewis was called up to the bridge conference room to meet with Yates and Edwards.

"Did you wish to see me sirs?" Lewis asked as he reported.

"Yes Doug, we did. Come on in and have a seat," invited Yates.

"How would you like to lead a recon patrol on the planet? Since we're in the neighborhood we might as well check out each planet we come across. Who knows, we may even find out the plight of the NOVAED crew," Yates alluded to.

"Sounds like a great picnic. I'm starting to get a little bit of cabin fever. Sure, I'd love to get outside for a while," Lewis replied.

It was planned the next morning Lewis would lead a flight of three Golden Hawks and explore the planet's surface. If the atmosphere proved to be friendly they would gather samples and bring them back to the labs for analyses. Otherwise they would shoot video of the planet as they flew over it.

The following morning at 0700 hours, LCDR Lewis left, launching his patrol from CONSTAELLATION. He was in the lead F-56-A, followed by two additional Golden Hawks.

"S.C.-1, S.C.-1 from Hawk-1 over," Lewis called the ship

"Hawk-1 this is S.C.-1. Go ahead with your traffic sir," LTJG Lister replied from the bridge communication station.

S.C.-1, we have departed CONSTELLATION and are proceeding down to the planet's lower atmosphere. Over," reported Lewis.

LTJG Lister replied, "I roger that Hawk-1, good luck."

The patrol made it down to a cruising altitude and the pilots were quite surprised by the magnificence of the spectacle before them. The sky was a light fuchsia in color that contrasted immensely with tall mountains made of crystal pillars of illuminated green, yellow, and blue reflecting the suns rays. They resembled an entourage of generously proportioned flashing neon signs. Several of the crystal-like marvels contained large openings inside their stature big enough for the patrol to fly through.

The Golden Hawks flew for miles over this wonderland, not a word was spoken by any pilot, they were left speechless by this brilliant sight. Captain Yates, now becoming concerned he hadn't heard from the flight ordered LTJG Lister to radio the patrol for a status report.

"Hawk-1, Hawk-1, this is S.C.-1 over," Lister repeated the call several more times.

"S.C.-1, This is Hawk-1 over," Lewis radioed back.

"Hawk-1, status report on the patrol over," Lister replied.

"There is no atmosphere down here suitable for us, however the sights are spectacular. The only thing going through my head right now is 'Lucy In The Sky With Diamonds". You know that old Beatles tune. Hell, wish I had some grass. Over," Lewis rationalized.

"Hawk-1, this is Yates, remember you're on a mission, not a trip. Any way to bring back specimens of the rock formations? Over." Yates asked.

"S.C.-1, there is no place to land down here. The entire surface is like the inside of a cavern. We're shooting as much video of the planet as we can. It should make for a very delightful Friday night home video presentation. Over," Lewis replied.

"We roger that. Advise when you're done tripping. S.C.-1 out," Yates sarcastically quipped.

The patrol continued on for several hours more, viewing the awesome extravaganza of the crystallized wonder.

Lewis radioed the other pilots "O.K. boys, let's call it a day and head for the barn".

The pilots raised the nose of their craft upwards to reach the mother ship. After the Hawks were secured on the hanger deck, Lewis took the video cartridges from each of the war birds and headed up to the bridge.

Yates, Edwards, Fisher and the rest of the science departments viewed the footage in the bridge conference room. Everyone was amazed at the sights of the planet's surface. Being there was no place to land and explore this wonder of nature, Yates ordered the ship to leave its orbit and proceed on its last heading. This course would cross the orbital path of the next inner planet of the system Antoric - 15. The journey would take about three days. Perhaps this planet would provide a friendly atmosphere, allowing the crew some enjoyment time to stretch their legs.

At the end of the third day CONSTELLATION reached her objective, she was in orbit around the 15th planet of the Antoric system. Observations of the planet from the orbit showed the planet was one massive storm. The storms were so severe a manned flight into the atmosphere would be too dangerous. A probe was launched and its reading of the planet's gasses showed it contained a great quantity of sulfurs and other elements fatal to humans. The star cruiser promptly left it's orbit of this planet and continued her trek inwards. Antoric -14's orbital path was well behind the ship so her next port of call would be Antoric -13, almost a week away.

Commander Edwards quizzed the captain.

"Al, are you sure you want to go to number 13? It could be bad luck, if we were of the superstitious nature."

"Now Ralf, are you afraid of the legend of the number? Here you are, a graduate of Annapolis, a veteran of countless conflicts, the executive officer of the most technologically advanced ship of mankind. And you're telling me a little superstition is going to keep you from exploring a new world," Yates humorously replied.

"You know, why take a chance. A superstition basically started as a rumor and we know rumors all contain some truth," Edwards sheepishly countered.

The captain looked dumbfounded and asked for the chart of the system. He took out his pen and wrote on the chart and then looked over to his comrade and said,

"Ralf, your point is well taken. I just renamed the planet Antoric-12 Bravo. This executive decision should take away any bad omens lingering around the subject matter" Yates contended.

Edwards looked at the captain and laughed, then said, "I'm ready for a cup." Yates advised LCDR Hall he had the com and the two men went off for a break and a cup of java.

CONSTELLATION'S travel to Antoric-13 now renamed Antoric-12 Bravo, went fast. The crew was busy engaged in training activities and regular duties. As the planet drew closer Yates requested LCDR Lewis to launch a recon patrol to check out the suitability of the planet's atmosphere. Lewis used his fastest fighters, the ASC-1's. He and a second ship left Connie and made way to the planet. As they entered the planet's outer atmosphere they advised the CONSTELLATION they were making their run.

The two ships entered the planet's atmosphere without incident, descending lower until they had a good vantage point to the planet's surface. The globe was very much like earth. The trees and foliage were reminiscent of the world they had left behind. The patrol scouted out an area by the coast line. It contained a perfect landing area for Connie to land safely. Lewis dropped a marker beacon so the area could be found by the mother ship, then they headed back up to make radio contact with CONSTELLATION.

"S.C.-1, S.C.-1, this is ASC-1 over," Lewis called.

"ASC-1, this S.C.-1. Go ahead with your report. Captain Yates is listening, over," LTJG Lister answered.

"Captain, we found a great vacation get away. How does a subtropical resort on the coast sound? There is a rock formation about one mile long and a quarter mile wide, perfect for Connie to land on and its right on the beach. Over," Lewis radioed.

"Sounds great Doug, I think we are all ready for some fresh air. Any sign of local inhabitants? Over," Yates inquired.

"Not as of yet, we just cruised the coast line, thought you might like to be near some water. The beaches look like those in Florida, nice and clean with white sand. We dropped the beacon and it is sending a homing signal, over," Lewis added.

"We roger that. We should be there in a few hours. If you guys

want to land and start a fire on the beach feel free to do so. I want you guys to stay together. Over," Yates concluded.

"Understood sir, we will be sitting on the beach sipping margaritas waiting for you. ASC-1 out," Lewis finished.

Yates called for a short meeting of all department heads. He advised Connie would be landing on the planet and didn't want a repeat of what had happened with the last vacation resort CONSTELLATION visited. He had the department heads talk to their personnel, NO ONE WAS TO GO OFF ALONE and all crew members would be armed.

CONSTELLATION picked up the marker beacon and headed to its mark. The star cruiser made a perfect descent through the atmosphere and found her landing site with no trouble. The surface of the rock tarmac was as smooth as any she had landed on. Over time the surface of the formation was worn smooth by the wind blowing sand over it.

After Connie rolled to a stop the hatches and hanger bay doors were cracked open. Yates and Fisher were the first ones to step off the ship. LCDR Lewis and the other pilot met them as they stepped off the ship. As the four men walked in the warm sunshine to the front of the ship Yates took deep breaths of the salty air and commented.

"The salt smells good. I am pleased with your findings Doug."

"Thank you sir. There are plenty of paths to make it down to the beach, the crew should have a good time playing on the beach. We took the liberty of testing out the water. It's just like Florida," Lewis replied.

"Yes indeedy. This is nice," Fisher injected. "Al, I'm going to get with Hall and Webb and get some sort of security perimeter set up. Do you want Edwards to release the children for recess?"

Yates agreed to the security measures and also o.k.'d the crew to indulge themselves. Yates and Lewis turned around to observe the inland side of the area. The rock formation on this side butted up against an area of white sand and gave way to rich tropical foliage. Wildlife could be seen frolicking under the green umbrella, which gently swayed from a soft breeze coming off the water. The trees provided a cool haven and brightly colored birds soared above its roof top. Within minutes members of the crew could be heard laughing as they made their way down to the beach and splashed in the warm bluish water. The rumble of the M-1 Abrams Battle tanks drowned out the party sounds as they rolled down the ramps of Connie to provide a security barrier. The tanks positioned themselves along the land side of the ship from the bow to the stern. Connie's upper and lower gun turrets were turned to face the seaward side of the ship.

Lieutenant Paul Atkins was ordered by Col. Fisher to take a foot patrol out to explore the jungle adjacent to the ship. The men, armed with their M-16 rifles headed into the thick undergrowth looking for any tell tale signs of trouble.

"Look sharp men, remember what happened the last time we let our guard down," Atkins ordered.

After two hours of traipsing through the jungle the tired patrol stopped to rest by a stream. One soldier who was hot and sweaty dropped his gear on the ground and ran to the stream and jumped in to cool off. Private Graves splashed around for a few minutes and then climbed out after SGT Royce told everyone to saddle up and get going.

The patrol scouted the area without incident and started to head back to the ship. The star cruiser just came into sight when Graves complained to his sergeant about his skin - it felt like it was burning. Royce told him it was probably the heat and to quit bellyaching about it. The scouting party was just walking up to the rock formation when Graves felt he was burning up. He took off his shirt and yelled,

"Holy shit!"

Atkins and the rest of the men in the patrol turned to see what the problem was. Graves was standing there in shock. His body was beet red and his skin was peeling off in layers. There was a film covering him and black sores were oozing. Atkins radioed the ship that he had a medical emergency just off the tarmac. Medical teams arrived and placed Graves on a stretcher and took him to sick bay.

By the time Dr. Jagman examined him, the entire body was covered with a fine white fungus. Graves was having difficulty breathing. LCDR Wang came in to help. She started taking specimens of the fungus in hopes of identifying it and finding a cure to combat it.

Yates was notified of the emergency and came down to sickbay, along with Col Fisher. LT. Atkins and SGT Royce gave their report of the patrol and noted that Royce was the only one who had gone swimming in the stream. Yates got on the ship's P.A. system and ordered everyone who had gone swimming to report to sickbay for observation, and that for the time being swimming was prohibited. The crew was checked out and no one seemed to exhibit symptoms of the ailment that was eating away at Grave's flesh. The antibiotics had no affect on the fungus. Jagman and Wang concluded it had to be something in the fresh water stream. The crew members who had swam in the salt water were healthy as could be. LCDR Wang called the captain and explained Jagman's and her hypotheses. She wanted permission to go down to the beach and get some sea water and to have someone bring back a container of water from the stream so she and Jagman could perform tests on them. Permission was granted and within an hour Wang was analyzing the water samples. The samples from the beach tested out fine, but the fresh water sample contained a bacteria, the same bacteria that was eating away the flesh on Private Graves.

Jagman and Wang were working relentlessly to find a cure. Graves was starting to slip away.

"Laura, let's drop a sample of the fresh water into the salt water and see if it has an effect on the bacteria. The crew who swam in the salt water did not show any signs of the contamination. Perhaps the salt in the water or something else kills it," Jagman quizzed.

"Dave, you might be right. There is not much time left, let's do it," Wang replied.

They mixed the two samples and then examined it under the microscope. The bacteria was dead. Jagman took a beaker containing the salt water over to the infected soldier and poured it over Graves' right arm. Within seconds the fungus on his arm turned to a fine white powder.

"That's it. The salt in the water kills the fungus. Call the captain and Col Fisher. Have them fill up two five gallons jugs and bring them here," Jagman ordered.

While the water was being retrieved from the beach Jagman and Wang moved Graves into a stainless steal tub. Yates and Fisher arrived with the salt water and Jagman poured it over his patient. The redness started to dissipate and normal skin color started to return. Vital signs began to improve and Graves started to breathe a little easier.

"As soon as the sores start to scab over, I'll start a salt solution I.V. Looks like old Danny Boy will be around with us for a while," Dr. Jagman said with relief.

Jagman had one of his staff prepare a fresh clean bed for Graves. While that was being done he explained to Yates and Fisher about the bacteria they had found in the fresh water. The ocean was safe, but caution should be used when near fresh water. He would experiment with salt tablets that could be used by foot patrols to ward off the effects, should they run into additional contaminated areas. Yates lifted the swimming ban on the beach and the following day the sun worshipers were back enjoying themselves.

Yates was down on the beach kicking back watching the waves break on the shore line when Fisher came up behind him.

"Mind if a land lubber joins you?" he asked.

"Colonel Fisher, sit yourself down. And might what that be in your canteen?" Yates asked.

"I think you know what this might be, have a swig," Fisher offered.

The captain tilted his head back and took a drink.

"I bumped into Jagman on the way out here. I congratulated him on finding a cure for Graves. He done a good job on this one Al," stated Fisher.

"The kind of thing your man ran into could happen back on earth, Just as long as we don't run into any more of those slug bastards, I'll be happy." Yates replied.

The two men sat back and enjoyed the scenery of female bikini clad crew members running up and down the beach when they heard their names being called. It was Commander Edwards. He made it up to them and sat himself down on the sandy beach.

"What is it Ralf?" Yates asked.

"Lewis just came back from is daily fun flight (meaning a re-con patrol). It looks like he may have found the remnants of the NOVAED crew," Edwards relayed.

"Really, where did LCDR Lewis find them at?" Fisher inquired.

"About one hundred and fifty miles northwest of here. He and

Lister are trying to translate what's left of the handwritten log now," Edwards replied.

"Well, let's go and see what they have," Yates said.

The three men headed back to the ship and found LCDR Lewis and LTJG Lister busy working on the log.

"Find anything out yet?" Yates asked.

LTJG Lister looked up from her work and spoke, "Yes sir, it sounds like the NOVAED briefly ran into the nebula which caused some mirror damage to the ship and some of the crew came down with radiation poisoning. Then they headed into the Antoric system. That's where they ran into trouble. I can't make out what planet it came from, but they were attacked by several ships from the inner planets. I'm thinking Antoric nine or ten."

"Well that is certainly something to look forward too," Edwards replied.

"We'll rest up here for a couple of days and when we head further in, we won't be caught by surprise like the NOVAED was. At least we have some warning of possible hostilities. Doug, take LCDR Wang back to the site and have her dig around it. She may be able to cough something else up. That's her field of expertise," Yates ordered.

Lewis and Wang took one of the shuttle craft back to the remains of the NOVAED crew. As she was sifting through the earth she found a pouch. The pouch contained a devise that she had seen before. It was a portable recording log Letam had used back on Zelcor.

"EUREEKA!" she exclaimed. "I think we have found what we came for."

It was starting to get late in the day so they headed back to Connie. Once aboard, Wang and Lister went to work on the electronic log. When they retrieved the information from it they summoned Yates to the lab.

"Captain, indeed the NOVAED was attacked, unprovoked. The incident occurred by Antoric-9. The ship was badly damaged and they were boarded. Some of the crew was taken prisoners, but the intruders were beaten back and that's when the ship escaped and went into orbit around this planet. Her captain abandoned the ship when the life support systems started to fail and the crew lived out the rest of their lives here. They too had run into the flesh eating bacteria. However, it's not in all the streams. They noticed that if marine life was present in the water, it was safe to use. They never made it as far as the coast line," Wang reported.

"Thank you LCDR Wang and LTJG Lister. You have provided some very valuable information. I'll meet with the army side, Commander Edwards, LCDR Lewis and Hall. If they want to play games with us we will be ready for them," Yates responded.

Yates left the lab and assembled his combat team for a meeting. He advised of the incident that had taken place with the NOVAED and called for recommendations from the men.

"Captain, I suggest when we get near the area we send out two scouting patrols, one behind the other. If the first wave runs into trouble the second can sweep in and help the other out. This would give Connie a chance to go to battle stations well ahead of the alien contact," presented Lewis.

"Sir, did the log indicate any kind of identification signatures from the alien ships? If so we could enter them into the data banks. This too would give a prior heads up," LCDR Hall asked.

"LCDR Wang still has a lot more to study on the log. You may want to check with her after the meeting and tell her what you need'" Yates replied.

"Al, I guess I'll just have my boys double up on patrolling the ship.

I'll also have Webb get assault teams ready in case our new to be found friends want to dance," Fisher injected.

"Skipper, I looked over the charts and it is unfortunate, we have to go right by Antoric-9. The radioactive nebula fans out so we can't just leave here and head straight back to Jersey," Edwards added.

"Ralf, are you sure it's not Jersey that fans out?" Yates jokingly asked.

The plans were set in case CONSTELLATION ran into trouble on the path ahead. The crew would remain on the planet for two more days then resume her travels.

The officers and crew enjoyed their last two days of exercises and relaxation on the planet, basking in the sun, swimming and hiking. The time went fast and now it was time to secure the ship's hatches and head back up into space.

The bridge crew reported to the captain, all departments were ready and the ship was secured. The order was given and CONSTELLATION turned around on the stone tarmac. She increased her speed and soon she was air borne. The star cruiser left the orbit of Antoric-13 and headed towards the inner planets.

Yates and Edwards left the bridge to go up to the officers mess for a cup of coffee. As they walked down the ship's corridors, they commented to each other how rejuvenated the crew looked. The short vacation was a boost for the ships morale.

As they were having their coffee and talking LCDR Lewis walked up to their table and sat down.

"Good, I finally caught up with you guys," Lewis said.

"What's on your mind, Doug?" Yates asked.

"Sir, we just passed Antoric-11 and I would like to start sending out patrols," Lewis replied.

"That's not a bad idea. The planets 9,10 and 11 are fairly close to each other, we may be being watched as we speak. Doug, get your boys ready. Ralf let's get back to the bridge," Yates recommended.

Yates ordered the ship to throttle back to half speed as the first group of fighters took off, leaving the ship behind them.

"Captain, some of Colonel Fisher's men have volunteered to assist in the gun mounts. I think this would be a good time to give them some training, if hostilities are looming on the horizon. Request permission to proceed with it?" Hall asked.

"Good plan Randy. If you're going to do it now, send Washington up here to man the weapons station. I want it manned at all times while we are in this star system," Yates replied.

LCDR Hall called Washington to replace him. As soon as Washington arrived on the bridge Hall left to conduct the training.

"Mr. Washington, how nice it is to have you up on the bridge. I can rest easier now, having you in my sight and knowing what you are doing," Yates ribbed.

"Sheet, this beats being down in that bingo parlor. Hell, dat place has turned into Brother Loves traveling Salvation Show. The preacher has used his evil Irish leprechaun powers and has changed my slots into them kettles you see around Christmas time. Very insulting to a man like me," Washington babbled.

"Did I hear the BINGO king here on the bridge?" Edwards asked as he walked in from the search center.

"Don't you bingo king me. Sheet you just wait till I get off this rust bucket. I'm gonna be the master of Atlantic City, then you be looking to me for pity. And that my friend is the niddy gritty and it's gonna be pretty. Sir," Washington blabbed.

"Ah, do I sense some anger? Perhaps we should schedule you for a counseling session with Father Delaney. He can help you with that you know," Edwards shot back.

Washington shook his head and sat down at his station Yates and Edwards chucked about his little outburst.

"Mr. Washington, I assume LCDR Hall explained your assignment to you. I want to know the exact second you have anything else on your screen besides our patrols," Yates ordered.

"Yes sir, he did. I'm on it, so don't have a fit. Ill let you know if I see any shit," Washington acknowledged.

Washington kept a close eye on his screen, as did the search center staff. So far the only thing showing was the two patrols some distance out in front of the ship.

The time passed slowly for Washington, who was use to being able to move around up on his feet working. He was having trouble staying awake. As he started to drift off he noticed a new blip on his screen. Not quite sure if he was imagining it, he wiped his eyes and took another look.

"SHIT! Captain Yates, I have a booger, I mean a bogie on the starboard beam of the first wave!" he yelled.

Yates and Edwards hurried to his station. Commander Edwards called the search center to confirm if it was a ship or a natural phenomena, the reply he got back was the target was under its own power and running straight.

"Al, Williams confirmed it is a ship, headed this way," Edwards reported.

"Lieutenant Lister, notify LCDR Lewis he has a target bearing 0-9-0 degrees off his starboard beam. Helm, full speed ahead. Mr. Washington this will be a first for you. Bring CONSTELLATION to battle stations." Yates barked out orders.

"BATTLE STATIONS, BATTLE STATIONS, THIS AIN'T NO DRILL FOOLS. BATTLE STATIONS, BATTLE STATIONS, ALL HANDS MAN YOUR FUCKING BATTLE STATIONS, HOP TO IT BITCHES!!!! Washington announced over the P.A. system.

Washington pressed the alert button. GONG, GONG, GONG, GONG blared out through the entire ship.

"How'd you like that sir, not bad for the first time ehh? Washington asked in a proud voice.

"No, Tyrone not bad for the FIRST time. I'll get you a script so you can study it," Yates replied.

"Captain, I contacted LCDR Lewis. He advises his air group is turning to meet the U.F.O. He requested the third wave of fighters be launched and a fourth be put on standby," LTJG Lister reported.

"Very well, Ralf take over Air Ops," Yates ordered.

Edwards left the bridge as per the captain's orders. The ship had increased her speed and slightly veered to the right to close the distance between her and the fighter combat patrols on her starboard side.

Lewis and his patrol were closing in on the target. They now had a visual on it. He attempted to open communications with it, but the craft would not answer. Suddenly a bright flash that resembled a bolt of lighting came from the strange craft. The red, yellow and blue colored plasma charge made its way to one of the F-56-A Golden Hawks, destroying it in a bright ball of fire.

Lewis ordered the remaining ships to disburse and attack the alien vessel on its port and starboard flanks. Yates, hearing of the destruction of one of the Hawks ordered all fighter craft to scramble. CONSTELLATION was brought to flank speed and the fight was on.

"CAPTAIN, I got all kinds of mother fuckers lighting up my screen. Shit there's 10, no 11, 12, must be 20 of them bitches on here now!" Washington exclaimed.

The Golden Hawks, once re-enforced still had their hands full. They paired off into two's to attack each target. It seemed as though when they destroyed one alien craft two more would pop up out of nowhere. Connie and the rest of the ship's air wing were now engaged in the heat of full battle. Every single gun and laser from the CONSTELLATION arsenal was being used to its maximum.

"Captain, the search center has informed me they have picked up over one thousand targets on the long range scanners, coming this way," LTJG Lister reported.

Captain Yates stopped in his tracks; his heart now racing was in his throat. He knew the odds of his ship coming out of this engagement were zero and the word massacre now stuck in his head.

"Thank you lieutenant, have Commander Edwards and Colonel Fisher report to the bridge on the double," Yates replied.

Within moments Edwards and Fisher arrived. They could tell by the expression on Yates's face things were not good. He asked them to join him in the conference room. All three sat down. There was a moment of grim silence.

"We are outnumbered and outgunned. Frankly we don't stand a chance. I'm going to order Lewis to pull his forces back and we'll try to make a run for it. Your thoughts gentlemen?" Yates asked in a despondent tone.

"Captain, I agree. But where do we run too?" Edwards asked.

"Al, I guess we have finally met our match. It's a pity I didn't get a chance to fuck with them on the ground. Kinda wish I knew what those bastards looked like. Sure would like to look the son of a bitch in the eye who is going to kill me." Fisher proudly replied.

"I'll give the order to pull back. Let's turn around and get all the birds back on board, when they are we will try to get the hell away from the alien vessels," Yates stated.

Yates, Edwards and Fisher walked back onto the bridge. Edwards and Fisher watched the battle on the main viewing screen as Yates went to the communications station and asked to speak to Lewis. Lister patched him through.

"Hawk-1 this is S.C.-1 Yates here. Doug, I want you to withdraw. There are too many of them. Connie is being turned around and will reduce speed. Have your birds come in on both sides of the ship. When you're all aboard, we're going to try and run for it. Over."

"Captain, I roger. I see what's coming at us. Looks like an ass kicking in the making," Lewis radioed back.

CONSTELLATION made her turn and the flock was following. Within a half hour the first of the fighters touched down inside the star cruiser's hanger deck. The deck crews worked feverishly to get all the craft secured, making room for the others returning.

"Captain, LCDR Lewis has advised his fighters have returned. The hanger bay is being secured at this time. He also advised his losses of seven birds," Lister relayed.

Yates shook his head in acknowledgement and ordered the ship to flank speed. The attacking ships from Antoric-9 were getting closer. Yates had to think of a way to buy his command some time and distance. He came up with an idea.

"Ensign Washington, how fast can you make ready four of the big birds for immediate launch?"

"Gonna nuke the mutha fuckers?" Washington asked.

“That’s right, we’re going to toast those fuckers all to hell,” Yates stated.

“Give me twenty minutes.  I know, you ain’t got twenty minutes. I’ll split the difference whit ya. How’s ten minutes sir?” Washington asked.

LCDR Hall entered the bridge and went directly to the weapons station. He and the Ensign entered the data into the control system it was ten minutes to the second they reported ready.

“Fire all four, spread them wide,” Yates ordered.

The ship jolted as the missiles left the launchers. The aft cameras were turned on and they waited for the detonations. Hall reported 600 targets were now within striking distance of CONSTELLATION. Things were tense on the bridge. If this last ditch effort didn’t work CONSTELLATION would come about and fight till her death.

KRARBOOM, KRARBOOM, KRARBOOM, KRARBOOM, all four missiles hit their targets. LCDR Hall reported all near targets destroyed. The onslaught of closing targets had slowed their speed for the time being, giving CONSTALLATION some breathing room and valuable distance.

CHAPTER 7

# USS ORION S.C.-2

While CONSTELLATION was being built in the Midwest, the navy and N.A.S.A. teamed upped and started to construct a second ship at the space center in Florida. Connie was built in a hurry to get the Space Command Unit underway and it was felt that the ship would be plagued with errors. The problems would be fixed at a later date when the simulated space flight mission was completed. The second ship was called the U.S.S. Orion S.C.-2 and it was planned the ORION would be the first ship of its class to make the first actual space flight to explore our solar system.

After contact was lost with CONSTELLATION, the construction of ORION was expedited. She was to be launched to search for her sister and if possible rescue her crew. A crew was assembled and a crash training program enacted for the men and women that would guide ORION through the stars. The ship was armed the same as her sister ship was when she left earth and she also had an air wing of

F-56-A Golden Hawk Fighters. ORION was equipped with an additional craft, the TS-1 Transport. This vessel could carry twenty passengers and their gear. She was armed with 50 caliber machine guns, air to air missiles and light lasers. With funds drawing tight, the army also got involved. They were very much interested in finding the armored detachment that was lost with CONSTELLATION and assigned personnel accordingly.

The ORION would be commanded by Captain Ken Meyers and her executive officer would be Commander Chris Page. Both were good friends of their counterparts, now missing in action. The army detachment would fall under the command of Colonel Mitch Reed who had served in many of the same conflicts as his friend Sam Fisher.

As ORION'S launch date drew closer her crew was on board making final preparations for the flight. There would not be the fan fare associated with the send off of CONSTELLATION'S simulated flight, but the spirit of all those involved was that of equaled excitement. Admiral Trout was on hand for the launch. He had a short meeting with Captain Myers just out side the hanger deck.

"Ken, I can't stress the importance of your mission. We have to find out what happened to CONSTELLATION and her crew. If we can't find answers, the entire space program may be in jeopardy. I wish you the very best of luck and smooth sailing. Please convey to the crew the army and the navy will take care of their families. I'll see you back in sixty days," Trout said.

"Don't worry admiral, we'll find out what happened. This mission has the best crew on board. Who knows, Al Yates is probably sitting on the moon sipping on some Jamisons," Meyers joked.

The two officers shook hands and Trout left the ship. Meyers went to the bridge to take command of the star cruiser. As he took his seat Commander Page advised him all departments had reported ready and the ship was pressurized.

"LCDR Finch, anytime you're ready, let's get ORION up into the cosmos," Meyers ordered over the phone.

"All ten are on line skipper, take her out of park and step on the gas," he replied.

The engines of the great ship roared and she slowly turned onto the taxi way. The star cruiser gathered her speed and soon she was airborne, making her way up to space. Within minutes ORION was in orbit above earth and the crew was busy checking all systems for glitches. None were reported. Meyers instructed LT Sue Randle to send a status report down to Space Command.

"Space Command Headquarters, this is ORION. All systems are go and we will be leaving orbit soon. Over."

"ORION, this is S.C.H. We roger your report. Good luck," was the reply.

"Chris, set a course for the last known coordinates of CONSTELLATION. It will be our starting point for a spiral search," Meyers ordered.

The data was entered into the helm control and the ship left earth's orbit, in search of her sister ship and fellow men.

The ORION passed the moon and her crew, like that of CONSTELLATION'S, were in awe of the sight. They studied each crater and every fold on its surface. Then, like earth it started to fade into the background of the dark cosmos star field. Captain Meyers turned the command over to his executive officer, Commander Page and made his way down to engineering.

"Mike how is everything doing down here?" he asked.

"Captain, welcome to my cave. Everything is working great. They built this ship damn good. I read over some of the status reports of CONSTELLATION, shit she was a disaster waiting to happen," Finch replied.

"That very well may have been her fate. If so, we should find some wreckage on Mars or debris orbiting the planet. It looks like things are in good hands down here. I need to stop in at Air Ops and chat with Mead. Let us know if you run into any problems," Meyers concluded.

Meyers stopped in at the air wing office and was advised LCDR Mead had taken a break and was at the officer's mess. Meyers thought he could use a cup of java and headed that way. As he entered he saw LCDR Mead sitting at a table looking through a porthole into space. Meyers was served his coffee and sat down to talk with him.

"Jack, I finally caught up with you. I just wanted to run over your plans for the Mars search," Myers said.

"Sir, good too see you. It's my understanding we will start a spiral search at the last known coordinates of CONSTELLATION. If nothing turns up there, I plan to send four Hawks and two TS-1's down to the planet and search its surface when we are close enough. By the way, I ran into LCDR Stout, she would like to check on the alien base CONSTELLATION made reference to in her report, time permitting," Mead stated.

"Looks to be a sound plan Jack, I think we could spare some time to check out the alien base. Who knows, those pirates from CONSTELLATION may have left something useful behind. Let me know if you need anything," Meyers replied.

The captain got up from the table and headed back to the bridge. On his way there he ran into Lieutenant Reginald Washington - he was the brother of Tyrone.

"Excuse me sir, do you have a minute?" he asked.

"Yes I do, what is it lieutenant," Meyers asked.

"Sir, it is my understanding a search of Mars will be conducted. If possible I would like to be part of the search team. My brother was on the other ship and I promised my mother I would help look for him," Reggie replied.

"Reggie, I don't see any problem with your request. I'll have LCDR Mead put you on the flight crew," said Meyers.

"Thank you sir, it means a lot to me. Somehow I think that scam artist is all right. Something tells me he is not dead."

Meyers proceeded back to the bridge and took over the watch. He had great anticipation that somehow his mission would find out the fate of CONSTELLATION. This captain was a firm believer in America's space program and it disturbed him deeply that Admiral Trout said 'the space program could be in jeopardy if no answers were found'. He would do his best to find the answers needed.

The day finally arrived. ORION was at the last known coordinates of CONSTELLATION and the search was to begin. The radar was fined tuned so it would pick up any metallic article, even one as small as a digital camera. Meyers gave the order and the ORION slowly turned in an ever-widening spiral circle. The mundane task was carried on 24 hours a day - they weren't going to miss anything. Several blips appeared on the screen and F-56A's were sent out to investigate every contact. These just proved to be asteroids heavy with metal ore. The search eventually took the star cruiser into the orbit of Mars. Thus the surface search was to be launched.

LCDR Mead led his small flotilla out of ORION consisting of 4 Golden Hawks and 2 transports. On board the TS-1's were LCDR Mary Stout, LT Washington and army security details. The smaller space crafts made it into the atmosphere of Mars without a single mishap and the ships spread out to conduct a wide search of the planet's surface.

Colonel Mitch Reed joined Captain Meyers on the bridge to observe the status of the mission.

"Good morning Ken. How are things progressing?" Reed asked.

"Hi Mitch, glad you could join the party. So far no problems and we're actually ahead of schedule. Mary and her group are just about to land at the alien base. I hope we can find some answers," Meyers replied.

The radio speaker cracked. It was LCDR Stout. "ORION, this is Science-1. We have just entered the base. From what we can see so far it looks like the CONSTELLATION done a fair job of stripping everything out of here. Over."

"Science-1, find out what you can. If they did leave anything useful we will make arrangements to bring it back on board. Good luck with your search," Meyers radioed back.

The science team carefully checked out the main room of the cavern, LT Washington was checking the area where the duplicating machines once stood. He noticed something on the wall. It was some writing, and as he read it he started to laugh. It read 'Tyrone was here' he chuckled out loud.

"That crazy mutha fucker. Spray painting his name all over New York ain't good enough for him. He has to do it on Mars too."

LCDR Stout heard him and walked over to explore the cause of the merriment. She chuckled too and looked over to Washington, who was wiping tears away from his eyes.

"Don't worry Reg, we will find him. I promise you that," Stout said to him.

Washington thanked her with his eyes and started to apologize, but she stopped him before he could start and just said in a very kind and soothing voice, "I understand".

Stout and Washington, accompanied by two soldiers entered the room that formerly housed the ASC-1 space craft. The room was empty except for a couple of stripped out craft. As they started to turn to leave, Washington saw a reflection on the wall.

"LCDR Stout, over there I saw something sparkle," Washington shouted.

They went over to investigate. It was a button partially concealed by dust. Stout inserted her fingers into it and a door slid open. The room lit up, revealing additional ASC-1 craft. They walked in to investigate the new-found marvels. The room also contained several duplication machines with spare parts for the space craft on them.

"ORION, ORION, this is science-1. It looks like the pirates didn't find everything. We have just discovered a cache of ASC-1's and duplicators. Over," Stout conveyed.

"Science-1 from ORION, I relayed your message to Captain Meyers. He advises well done. I'll contact LCDR Mead and have him meet with you at your location.

Over," radioed back LT Randle.

"We roger your transmission. And will be waiting for LCDR Mead. Science-1 out."

The find was certainly good news for Meyers, at least ORION would not return to earth empty-handed. Mead studied the ASC-1 reports that LCDR Lewis had transmitted back to earth and he and several of his fighter pilots self-trained on how to fly the new found treasures back to the ship. Work details moved the replication machines up to ORION, installed them, and in a short time had them in working order. The task kept the ORION in Mars' orbit for four days.

While the transfer of alien equipment was taking place, additional search teams were formed and managed to search the entire planet for any remnants or remains from CONSTELLATION. Nothing was found except for the handwriting on the cavern wall from Tyrone Washington.

ORION transmitted her reports of Mars back to Space Command Headquarters on earth. They also advised they would resume the space search the following morning.

At 0800 hours the following day Meyers met with his X.O Commander Page and drafted out a new search pattern. They would take ORION out past Mars and start a new grid so not to be re-searching the area they have already covered. The day of travel proved uneventful and Meyers was about to call it a day when the radar operator caught his attention.

"Captain, I have something weird on the screen."

"What is it Roy?" Meyers asked.

"I don't know sir, it looks funky," Ensign Keen replied.

"LT Randle have LCDR Finch report to the bridge immediately," the captain ordered.

She complied with the captain's request, and within minutes Finch reported.

"You rang sir?" Finch asked.

"Yes I did. Take a look on what Ensign Keen has on his screen. Could this be the remains of CONSTELLATION?" Meyers asked.

"Shit, I don't know. It could be the nuclear fuel from the engines emitting off radiation. Hell it's worth a look," Finch, shaking his head, replied.

Meyers had Keen send the coordinates over to the helm station and the captain ordered him to take the ship there. Meyers also called down to Air Ops to have a couple of fighters get ready to search the area. As the ship got closer to the target, the blip on the screen magnified at an alarming rate.

"Captain, we're increasing speed. The ship is now at three quarters and we're supposed to be at one quarter," the helmsman advised.

LCDR Finch muttered, "What the hell?"

He called down to the engineering office and asked if they were having any trouble. They reported none. The ship continued to increase speed. Meyers, who was now assisting Finch with the helm control's ordered Commander Page to bring ORION to general quarters.

GONG,GONG,GONG,GONG. "All hands general quarters, general quarters - this is not a drill!" Page announced over the P.A. system.

Some of the crew, awakened from sleep, ran to their duty stations half dressed. Page advised the captain all departments had reported ready and were awaiting further orders.

The ship was now running faster than what her engines would allow, even at flank speed. The fact of the matter was the engines were in full reverse, straining to hold back the forward momentum of the ship. Commander Page looked up at the main viewing screen and let out an "OH, MY GOD." In the center of the screen was a great big void in space. Stars could be seen bordering the outside of the circular opening, but the inside was just a foreboding black void.

The engines were now showing signs of strain - the vessel was shuddering and there was no steering control. The lights flickered and unsecured items flew throughout the ship, striking everything in its path and causing damage and injury.

The ship was being sucked into the black void of space. Panic ran amok inside the vessel. All efforts attempted by the crew were to ward off the abyss met with failure. The star cruiser was turning head over tail as she slipped into the void and finally disappeared, swallowed out of sight.

ORION was spit out on the other side of the hole. Captain Meyers, who had been knocked out when he fell to the deck, regained his composure and was helped back up to his feet by Commander Page. Meyers shook his head to ward off his grogginess and asked. "What the hell happened? Where are we?"

"I don't know sir, there doesn't seem to be too much working on board," Page replied.

LCDR Finch came to and echoed the same question as everyone else on the bridge.

"Skipper, I better get down to engineering to see what we have left."

"Chris, get on the horn, I want all department heads to meet in the bridge conference room in a half hour with status reports," Meyers ordered.

The X.O. advised the heads of each section of the captain's request and within the allotted time the department commanders reported for the meeting.

Myers opened the meeting with, "I don't know what has happened to us or where we are, we may have experienced the same fate of CONSTELLATION. Communications are down all across the board with earth. I need to know what kind of shape the ship is in before we do anything."

"Captain, if you would start with me, I have reports from the sick bay areas. They are swamped with injuries and I need to return as soon as I can. The wounded are lined up in the passageways. We don't know how many more are scattered around the ship. My assistance is badly needed," Commander Joe Crane, the ship's medical officer reported.

"Ken, my medics are available to help out in your sick bays and my men are at your disposal," Colonel Mitch Reed interjected.

"Thank you, Colonel. Doc, get with Commander Page or myself as soon as you know the extent of the crews injuries. Doctor, you may return to your duties," Meyers acknowledged.

"Sir, we have one engine online, Washington is in the process of getting the auxiliary generators fired up. We have enough power to sustain life support, that's about it. With any luck we should get the other mains on line soon," LCDR Finch reported.

The departments went down the line with their reports. LCDR Mary Stout reported she had damage in her area and a heavy loss of plants that were vital to sustaining oxygen levels in the ship. Her crew was working on salvaging what they could.

LCDR Mead advised he had little damage to his fighters and was disbursing his crews to help out the other departments.

Father Daniel O'Rourke, the ship's Chaplin advised he would be helping with the wounded in the sick bay area.

The captain requested hourly reports on repairs and other problems encountered. He dismissed the meeting and toured the ship to see the extent of the damage for himself. The ship was in a state of disarray. It looked as if a tornado had swept through it. Liquids had leaked out of containers and spread over many of the decks, creating a slippery hazard - broken glass and other materials were scatted into every nook and cranny in every compartment. Crews were busy extinguishing small fires that had swept throughout the ship. It would take days to restore the star cruiser to the order she was in prior to the incident that had just occurred.

Meyers returned to the bridge and informed his X.O. on the state of the ship. Little by little over the next two days the ship's systems returned to normal operating status. By the fourth day Finch and Washington had managed to get many of the main engines back on line. Most of them were up to par, but several of them still needed minor adjustments.

Meyers and Page held a meeting with LCDR's Stout, Finch, Mead and LCDR Bert Adams, the weapons/security officer, about what their options were. It was agreed they should travel forward. They didn't know which direction they had come from and drifting in space would not achieve anything.

Meyers gave the order to proceed forward at one half speed and to start a plot from the current coordinates when the navigation's computer came back online. The ORION had now suffered the same fate of her sister, the CONSTELLATION.

CHAPTER 8

# THE ANTORIC EXPERIENCE TIMES TWO

ORION now had all of her engines fully operational. Most of the repairs and cleanup from the ordeal were complete, leaving mostly little touch-up jobs to be finished. Nothing had been reported out of the ordinary for the past two days and the crew were starting to settle in for what would be a longer than planned voyage.

Myers and Page were up in the officer's mess having coffee and a bite to eat when Colonel Reed stopped in to join them.

"Figure out where were are at yet, Ken?" Reed humorously asked.

"No, not yet. I suspect we're someplace off the east coast, perhaps by L.A," Meyers jokingly replied.

"If rumor has it correct, they'll be sending up a third ship to find out what happened to us," Page added.

"Now what do you know about the supposed third ship of this class?" Meyers asked.

"I overheard Admiral Trout, when I was in D.C. last month. He was bitching about the contractors bitching about not everyone getting a fair shake in the building of these marvelous wonders so to appease the contractors a third ship was ordered," Page answered.

An announcement came over the P.A. System. "Captain and X.O. to the bridge."

"Care to join us Colonel, sounds important?" Meyers asked.

The three men hurried to the bridge, where they saw LCDR Adams and Ensign Keen looking at the radar screen.

"What's up?" Meyers asked.

"Captain, we just had four large blips appear on the radar screen for a split second. From my training it resembled nukes going off," Adams replied.

"Nukes, I thought we were the only idiots in the universe to have those things," Reed responded.

"Can you play it back?" Meyers asked.

The ensign ran the back-up file on the blips and Adams compared them to file images from the data banks. Everyone agreed they were the echoes of nuclear explosions. The captain ordered the ship's speed reduced and called down to air operations. He wanted some scouts out in front of the ship. LCDR Mead led a patrol of four Hawks, positioned some four thousand yards off of ORION'S bow.

On board the CONSTELLATION Captain Yates was fighting the battle of his life and for the lives of his crew. The enemy craft from

Antiric-9 had only paused in their attack for a brief moment. They were now advancing at a rapid pace.

"Al, there is a large asteroid up ahead, we could use it to conceal a counter attack," Commander Edwards relayed.

"Ralf, at this point in time it doesn't seem to make any difference. Those bastards will be all over us real soon. Let's give them a fight. Call down to Lewis and have his boys get ready. As soon as we are on the far side of it we'll launch everything we have and go out in a blaze of glory," Yates responded.

CONSTELLATION, while fighting off single ship attacks managed to make her way to the far side of the asteroid to launch her fighters. As the war birds were leaving the hanger deck to get into battle formation the long range sensors picked up a large blip and four smaller ones on their screens.

"Captain, looks like we have company off the starboard side," LCDR Hall stated.

"Fuck, how the hell did they get there! The bastards beat us to the punch. Launch a couple of nukes to take care of them. Save the rest for the other ass holes," Yates blared out.

"MY GOD, hold it sir," Hall exclaimed.

"What is it, make it fast Randy. The enemy fleet is coming at us faster than hookers going down to the piers on navy day," Yates insisted.

"Captain, the ship's signatures, they resemble... well they resemble ours," Hall replied.

"What, why that can't be. Are you sure?" Yates asked.

"He's right Al, they're the spitting image of ours. Hell I'm confused. You suppose our friends out there would hold off the attack until we could investigate?" Edwards questioned.

"Wishful thinking Ralf. LT. Lister, send a message to that ship out there advising them of our identity lets just hope to hell there not Viron looking for a rematch," Yates ordered.

Lister sent the message. "To unidentified ship, this is the earth star cruiser U.S.S. CONSTELLATION. Please identify yourself." Lister repeated the message several more times, and had no reply.

"Captain Meyers, I'm receiving a message from CONSTELLATION," LT. Randle shouted in a surprised voice.

"Are you sure Lieutenant? CONSTELLATION?" Meyers questioned.

She confirmed to the captain that it was the lost star cruiser. Captain Meyers then ordered her to patch him through to CONSTELLATION.

"CONSTELLATION, this is the U.S.S. ORION, Captain Ken Myers commanding. Over."

"Captain Yates, Captain Yates, I have a reply. They say they are the U.S.S. ORION, a Captain Ken Meyers is in command," Lister shouted.

"Ken Meyers, son of a bitch ORION, my god they built a second ship. Patch me through lieutenant," Yates ordered.

ORION had just picked up the CONSTELLATION and the asteroid on her radar at the same time the speakers on her bridge squawked.

"Ken, this is Al Yates, you got here just in time for the party. We are at battle stations getting ready for a counter attack on about a thousand little green bastards coming at us. If you're not doing anything at the moment you're more than welcomed to join in," Yates radioed.

"Alex, it seems you find yourself getting into trouble even out in space. We were about to break for lunch, so if you could hold off for a while we may be able to join you, say in an hour or two," Meyers replied.

"Ken, I sure wouldn't want to upset your lunch plans, but things are getting a little hot right now," Yates responded.

"Hold on for a couple Al, we're going to battle stations now," Meyers conveyed.

"Commander Page, bring ORION to battle stations," Meyers ordered.

"Aye sir, BATTLE STATIONS, BATTLE STATIONS, ALL HANDS MAN YOUR BATTLE STATIONS, THIS IS NOT A DRILL," Page announced.

GONG, GONG, GONG, WHOOP, WHOOP, WHOOP. The alarm sounded through the ship. The ORION was going to help her sister who was in desperate need of assistance.

Meyers ordered the ORION to make flank speed as she headed to CONSTELLATION. At the same time she launched her entire complement of fighters.

ORION rendezvoused with CONSTELLATION behind the asteroid. Yates had already formulated a new battle plan. He hailed his sister ship.

"Ken, we don't have much time, the little green bastards are getting close. On my mark, bring your ship to the top of the asteroid. We are going to fire four nukes, if you'll fire four also that should stop them in their tracks. After detonation we'll rush them with all the fighters and the mother ships. Then chase them all the way back to Newark," Yates proposed.

"Al, I think eight nukes should blow them all the way back to Jersey. I'll wait for your word," Meyers replied.

Both star cruisers maneuvered to the top of the asteroid and were covered by an umbrella of Golden Hawks and ASC-1's. Yates counted down to the launch of the big nuclear armed missiles. As soon as he said "fire" the star cruisers sent four missiles each towards the attacking green ships from Antoric-9. Both captains tracked their birds on the radar screens. They watched as the eight large blips rushed into a solid wall of smaller blips.

Both ships shuddered as the eight heavy explosions rocked their vessels. The entire region was lit up like a Yankee Stadium at a night game. The radar screen went blank for a few minutes as the targets were obliterated. Then blips slowly started to reappear.

"Ralf, we're going in for the kill, anything you want play?" Yates asked.

"As a matter of fact, yes I do." Edwards inserted a CD into the communications consol and said, "Lieutenant Lister, if you would be so kind to blast this over the air waves after the captain gives the attack order, I would be most appreciative," Edwards politely asked.

"Yes sir, I would be happy to assist you with the broadcast. Captain, the radio is yours," Lister replied.

"Attention all units. The time has come to push these little green devils from our path. Good luck and kick ass. CHARGE!" Yates commanded.

As soon as his words left the ship, LT Lister flipped the switch and the music from the CD started to play. The entire task force left the asteroid with guns blaring and missiles headed out in front to the tune 'AFTERNOON DELIGHT'. Yates looked over to his X.O. and questioned in a disgusted voice.

"AFTERNOON DELIGHT, Ralf, really?"

"Sorry captain, I was in a rush and must have grabbed the wrong CD." Edwards replied.

Yates's battle strategy proved good. The forces from earth were now starting to prevail in the conflict. The enemy fleet was starting to falter and their advance was all but stopped. CONSTELLATION, re-enforced from ORION, was beating the enemy in their own back yard and several formations of the Antoric vessels were starting to fall back. One crippled enemy ship was close to CONSTELLATION, and Yates wanted a prisoner. With nearly all the air crews involved in combat, air crews on board were scarce.

"Ralf, take the com, Mr. Washington come with me. We're going fishing and you just got volunteered. That cripple over there – we're going to bring her aboard," Yates ordered.

"Sheet, you gotta be out of your mind sir. Let's just blast that mutha to kingdom come. Sheet, you wanna go out there and bring back those little Keeblers! That's all we need - a bunch of little green leprechauns running around this bucket," Washington replied.

Yates and his unwilling victim fired up one on the transports and steered towards the crippled vessel. As they closed in on it, the ship opened fire, using up the last of its dwindling power.

"Cappy, that green cracker is shooting at us. Get me a little closer so I can kick that green motha fucking munchkin's ass," Washington stated.

"Don't worry, Tyrone. When we get these crackers on board, you can have your way with them. I'm appointing you as the official ambassador to the Antoric Empire," Yates replied.

Washington sat back in his chair with a big grin on his face. Yates maneuvered the shuttle craft to the aft end of the disabled ship and latched onto the small but deadly vessel. The shuttle craft then pushed it back to the CONSTELLATION. As soon as both craft were secured on the hanger deck, the door was slid shut. Colonel Fisher was ready with an armed security detail to greet the Antoric visitors. The captured craft's occupants would not unseal the hatch and come out. LT Lister came to assist by bringing down a translator box, but without the cooperation of the guest, it was to no avail.

Yates looked over to Colonel Fisher and said, "Sam perhaps you and your boys could persuade our new friends to come out and join us for tea."

"Why Alex, isn't that just mighty neighborly of you. I'll be more than happy to give them critters a good dose of southern hospitality," Fisher replied.

Fisher gave his men the order to fire their M-16 weapons into the hull of the ship. The squad fired several short blasts, but still no response.

"Sheet, I know a way to drive those little green jeans out of there. Everyone grab a crow bar or some of them other tools over there. We'll give those chumps one hell of a head ache," Washington instructed.

Each person, including Yates and Fisher picked up a metal tool or rod and started to pound the outside of the green ship. The pace quickened and became more forceful as the men started to actually vent rage and frustration from the ongoing battle. As they pounded on the craft, they volleyed a fire ball of yelling and screaming at the occupants.

"Come out of there you little devil." "Open the fucking door." "Ding dong, Avon calling." "Your pizza is here bitch." "Support your local police, you're gonna give till it hurts." "Who said the police, they after me?"

The warriors started to enjoy themselves, the physical activity proved to be good medicine for their mental psyche. After ten minutes of pounding, the hatch cracked open. Fisher ordered his men to pick up their weapons and rush the opening. As they peered in, they saw two beings holding their heads as if they were having an Excedrin moment. The aliens were motioned to come out and they slowly stepped out of their craft onto the deck. The occupants stood four feet tall, with rounded heads and round eyes. They had short, stubby noses and no hair. The skin tone was that of a light olive green. And they were dressed in a silver colored space suit.

Washington blurted out, "Sheet, they aint keeblers, they be tella tubbies."

"These are the little bastards we are running from?" Yates questioned.

"Yo Al, you better let me have the first crack at these little green gummy people. After all bro, I is the ambassador," Washington insisted.

"Yo, Al? Getting a might bit informal, aren't we Mr. Washington?" Yates shot back with a disproving scowl.

The two prisoners were escorted to the air ops debriefing room to try and start working on the language barrier of the two races with the use of the translator box.

The phone rang and Yates answered it. It was Commander Edwards.

"What good news do you have for me, Ralf? " Yates asked.

"Captain, I am pleased to inform you, the little green hornets are in full retreat. What are your orders?" was the response from the other end.

"Keep pressing the little bastards," Yates replied.

He no sooner hung up the phone when the ship shuttered and a loud THUMP was heard. CONSTELLATION was hit. The general alarm was sounded, the smell of smoke prevalent in the air. Yates ordered the prisoners locked down in the brig and he rushed to the bridge. As he entered, he heard Commander Edwards Shouting orders to the weapons control consol operator.

"Train all guns off to starboard and fire. Randy, get a hold of Lewis and tell him we need a CAP over us now."

"What happened?" Yates asked.

"We were focused on the ships ahead of us. I didn't see the bastards' way off on the starboard side. They snuck in on us captain. ORION took a couple of hits too, captain," Edwards replied.

"Give me the damage report." Yates ordered.

Both ships took additional hits before the combat air patrol returned to destroy the aggressors. Damage to CONSTELLATION was minor; however ORION was a little more serious. It appeared the ambush by the Antoric ships was a desperate move to ward off the earth ships from pushing their forces back. Their attempt failed and the Space Command forces, once outnumbered, were starting to see a victory in sight.

LT. Lister called up to the bridge and notified the captain she had broken through the language barrier and was communicating with the Antoric prisoners. Yates though it would be a good time to find out what their problem was, as the fighters were returning for rearming and repairs. The radar screens were finally empty of enemy contacts.

Yates went to the brig area to meet with Lister and the prisoners. Fisher was also sitting in.

"What have they said, anything?' Yates asked.

"Sir, they say we are the aggressors. We have trespassed in their space, from what I can gather. They are a closed society and wish to have no contact with other races," Lister replied.

"Your synopsis, Sam," Yates asked.

"Hell Al, they won't talk to me. They only talk with Lieutenant Lister. I must have bad breath or something," Fisher replied.

"Carol, try to instill in their green little heads, we were only passing through. We have no intentions of hurting them or taking them over," Yates requested.

"Captain to the bridge, Captain to the bridge," called over the P.A. system.

Yates advised Lister and Fisher to try to convince the Antoric prisoners to contact their leaders to stop the fighting. This war was unnecessary. There was no justification for it. Yates returned to the bridge and was motioned over to the radar station.

"Looks like round four, captain. The green machines are massing in front of Antoric-9," LCDR Hall informed.

"Ralf, notify Lewis his services will be needed, and also let Captain Meyers know on the ORION," Yates ordered.

"Skipper, we can take them all out with another nuke attack," Hall stated.

"That may be an option, Randy. If we can convince our guests downstairs to tell their boss the hostilities can end, we may not have to use them," Yates replied.

Yates called down to LT Lister to see if she had made any more progress with the Antorics. She advised none. He then asked if there was enough data in the translator unit to broadcast a message to them. She advised there was and would be back on the bridge to set up the broadcast.

Yates then contacted Captain Meyers and unveiled his plan; option one was to use diplomacy, if that failed option two would be nukes and a full scale space and surface battle. Meyers agreed with the plans and would be standing by. His fighters were ready for launch when the word was given.

Lister hooked up the relay and Yates broadcast to the Antoric authorities.

"Attention Antoric rulers, I am called Alex Yates, captain of the earth star cruiser USS CONSTELLATION. I speak for this ship, as well as for the USS ORION. We have come in peace. We are trying to find our way home to earth. We have flown through your planetary system as part of our journey. We have not come to wage a war against your people or to take over your worlds. There is no need for further loss of life. If hostilities cease, we will leave your system and continue on our way. However, if you insist on fighting, we will prevail with victory. I urge you now for a cease fire. I will await your reply," Yates finished.

There was no answer from the Antoric's. The captain paced up and down the bridge, waiting for word that the war would be over. An hour had passed and still no reply.

"Ralf, do you think the translation got screwed up? Why haven't they answered?" Yates asked.

"I don't know Al, they haven't attacked. Perhaps they are discussing it," Edwards replied.

LCDR Hall interrupted. "Gentlemen I think we have our answer."

Yates and Edwards turned to him.

"Looks like a few more green hornets are joining the party. SHIT, they just took a pot shot. Should I return fire sir?" Hall asked.

"No, hold up a minute. They may be testing our word. If they shoot again, we'll retaliate," Yates countered.

Eyes were glued to the radar screen and to the main viewer, watching to see if it would be a continuation of war, or if there would be peace.

"Captain, Captain Meyers wishes to talk with you," Lt Lister reported.

"Very well, patch him through," Yates instructed.

"Al, looks to me they are still massing ships. If they get too organized we could be in trouble. ORION needs a few days in the yards. We still have some fight left in us, but we're not up to 100%," Meyers stated.

"Yes Ken, we've been watching. If they shoot again, let's hit them with a new barrage of nukes from both ships. That may get their attention and they may opt for a peaceful solution to this mess," Yates replied.

"I roger that. Just give the word. ORION out."

The standoff continued for a while longer. It started to run through Yates's head the enemy was just buying time to mass its forces in strength. His answer soon came.

"Captain, looks like they're going to make a run for us. Yep, they're laying down a fire pattern. We are still out of their range, now is the time to send them a birthday greeting," LCDR Hall advised.

"Inform ORION we launch the nukes in sixty seconds," Yates commanded.

The word was passed to the sister ship, and one minute to the second eight more nuclear missiles were launched towards the attacking forces.

Within minutes eight bright flashes brightened up the blackness of space and the reverberations shook CONSTELLATION and ORION. The attacking forces were once again decimated, with only a few surviving ships trying to continue the attack. Yates ordered the fighters be launched to mop up the intruders, with ORION following suit. LCDR Lewis radioed the ship and advised his radar had picked up a missile incoming from the planet's surface. For some unexplained reason, Antoric-9 was continuing with the battle. Captain Yates advised him to have his command destroy anything that left the planet's atmosphere.

With immediate danger to the star cruisers now a low level threat, Yates scheduled a meeting between the two ship's commanders for a ground assault on the planet. Captain Meyers and Colonel Reed were being shuttled over to CONSTELLATION for the summit.

Yates, Edwards and Fisher were waiting for their counterparts to arrive in the deck-6 conference room. The shuttle craft from ORION landed on the hanger deck. Meyers and Reed were escorted up for the meeting.

"Ken, how the hell are you? Damn glad you arrived when you did. You guys saved our asses. I think you know my X.O. Ralf Edwards, and this is Colonel Sam Fisher, commanding the army contingent on board," introduced Yates.

"Glad we could join in the festivities. Al, no matter where you go you always manage to get into some kind of trouble. I thought the reserve assignment would be a safe one for you. Let me introduce Colonel Mitch Reed, he is commanding the army detail on board my ship," Meyers replied.

"Mitch, you old Yankee son of a bitch, I haven't seen you since we left Baghdad. Compared to what we have been through on this mission, they seem like the good old days," Fisher declared.

"I see you two are old friends," Edwards added.

"Yes, we've been through a few scrapes together. Sam is a good old southern boy, as we called him back in the states," Reed joked.

"We better get down to business. It looks like those Antoric asses wish to continue the fight. I propose Connie's birds make a recon flight over the northern hemisphere and your fighters take the southern hemisphere. As they map out potential targets they could drop a few subtle hints on our little green friends that it is useless on their part to continue this conflict. Hopefully we can avoid a ground campaign," Yates explained.

"It would be nice if those varmints could get it through their fat little green heads we're going to whoop their asses. However, I think they've had a little too much moonshine to drink. I say we combine forces from both ships and concentrate our fire power on one target at a time. The use of overwhelming force does have its advantages," Fisher interjected.

"I agree with Sam. If we divide up and take on two targets at a time we risk being the weaker force and subject ourselves to defeat," Reed added.

"It would be easier providing a CAP over both ships at one location than two. It would free up aircraft for active combat," Meyers interjected.

"The only advantage we will loose is the element of surprise. They will see us as we come in to a L.Z. It's best if we act as one unit," Edwards concurred.

"Yeah, that was my feeling too. Let's start the recon operation, and when we get the data we need, pick out our targets and plan the raid," Yates concluded.

"One more thing gentlemen, I propose a toast to victory," added Yates.

He reached down under the table and pulled out a haversack containing Jamison's, ginger ale and ice. He mixed the liquids in five glasses. Each of the officers picked up their beverage and held it up. As they clinked glasses, they said in unison, "TO VICTORY" and drank up.

After the cocktails were consumed, Captain Meyers took Captain Yates aside and asked, "Al, do you have an enlisted man aboard named Tyrone Washington?"

"No, we don't," Yates replied with a smile on his face. He continued, "I have an Ensign Tyrone Washington in my crew, we promoted him up the chain because of the superb job he does. Why?"

"His brother is part of my crew. One of the reasons he volunteered for this mission was to find his brother," Meyers replied.

"Oh my God, the navy has two of them! Ralf, Tyrone's brother is on the ORION," Yates called out.

"This is certainly going to be an interesting journey from here on out. Two Washington's, I think I'm going to put in for retirement," Edwards answered.

The representatives of CONSTELLATION brought their visitors up to date on the antics of their beloved Tyrone. The laughter was at times loud as they heard of his deeds. Yates and Meyers concocted a scheme to reunite the two brothers. Tyrone was to go back to ORION with Reed and himself on the false pretence their weapons officer was ill and Washington would fill in until he recovered.

As the shuttle was getting ready for its return trip, Washington was called to the hanger deck and told of his assignment.

"What's you doing always volunteering me for? Sheet, can't get no rest on this bucket, now I have to baby-sit two buckets? I got slot machines to care for. Hell, with me gone the money is gonna walk out the door and then I'll be poor and have to sleep on the floor and that makes me sore," Washington gripped.

"See what I mean Ken?" Yates asked.

The shuttle returned to the ORION with Washington on board. When it was safe to enter the hanger bay, an officer walked out and Washington uttered, "Hell at least you have brothers on board this tub. HEY, HEY, THAT IS MY BROTHER! Tyrone yelled. He jumped out of the craft and continued, "REGGIE, REGGIE, what you doing up here, you sorry mutha. Sheet, I'm glad to see you."

Both brothers ran into each others arm and hugged. It was very emotional.

"What do you mean calling me a mutha, mister. I am a lieutenant in the United States Navy. Remember that Ensign," Reggie replied in a harsh serious tone.

"Ahh, fuck you, I'm always getting that shit on that other boat and it gets my goat," Tyrone countered.

The two brothers laughed, patting each other on the back.

"Reggie, take some time and spend it with your brother. Show him around the ship if you want. Take all the time you need," Meyers stated.

The brothers toured the ship and sat down and talked for hours about old times, family, and the encounters in space. Reggie went back to the CONSTELLATION with Tyrone to see the upgrades on board and to place a visit to TYRONES PALACE.

The air recon patrols from both ships had returned and the commanders were in the air operations briefing room on board their respective ships studying possible targets, for it looked like a massive ground battle was looming in the near future. After viewing the video footage, the conversation turned to what the quickest and most decisive measure to take would be. A meeting was set up by telecommunications.

"I think if we could find out where the capitol city is from our little green friends downstairs, we should make it our prime objective," Fisher stated.

"I agree, Sam. However, I don't think we want to show them our hand right off the bat. Let's keep them confused. We can attack a couple of outer-lying cities first, let them think that is where we are attacking; then switch gears and strike the main target," Yates added.

"I think incorporating both scenarios sounds like the most attractive plan. Maybe throw in a left turn on it. Attack our secondary targets in daylight hours for a couple of days, and also try to take out any communications links. This should force them to concentrate their defenses away from the prime target. Then, on night three or four, land as close to the capitol as we can and hit them by surprise," Mead added.

"Sounds good, sounds tricky and its simple. I like it," Captain Meyers stated.

The war planning committee discussed the tactics further and fine tuned the plan through the ensuing hours. The offensive would be a go after Yates tried one more crack at diplomacy. Strategy and tactics were on the side of the earthlings, however, they still would be fighting a battle on the opposing team's home court and their weapons for the most part were still unknown variables that could change the outcome of victory.

Yates summoned LTJG Lister to the meeting to see if she had gained any more information from the prisoners.

"Carol, have the little green pea pods cracked open with anything yet?" he asked.

"I was up with them most of the night, I think I am making some headway with them and they understand we were just passing through their system. They are still very reluctant to communicate with their superiors and have them cease hostilities," she replied.

"Al, perhaps a little psychological warfare could play into the game now and help out our cause," Commander Edwards churned in.

"Perhaps Ralf, are you wanting to play AFTERNOON DELIGHT to them?" Yates shot back.

Everyone in the room chuckled at the remark. Commander Edwards continued on with his idea.

"Maybe that would work. I was thinking, let's show them our weapons and then show them videos on what the consequences would be to their home planet if we would have to use them against them. The devastation is far worse in an atmosphere than what they have seen in space."

"You know, if they have anything in their little heads it might soak through. It's an avenue certainly worth exploring. If this diplomatic measure works, then we are ahead in this game," Meyers said in agreement.

The meeting ended, Meyers and Reed signed off. Commander Edwards and LTJG Lister were assigned to convince the Antoric prisoners their people would not be the winners of a ground war. They were shown the videos of how destructive the weapons would be if they were used on the planet. The prisoners showed signs of horror as they figured out the effects of the tools of war that would be used by the people of earth, and they hesitantly started to cooperate.

Yates was notified of their willingness to help avert further war and he ordered the prisoners brought to the bridge. When they arrived, it was explained to them they needed to communicate with their leaders to end the war. Lister prepared the communications console for the task at hand. Via the radio, two prisoners pleaded with their superiors to come to terms and end all hostilities. The crew on the bridge listened to the broadcast with the help of the translator unit. The alien leaders called the two Antorics traitors and implied they had been brainwashed by their aggressive captors. It seemed the last chance of diplomacy had failed. The two Antorics were taken back to their holding cells to await the outcome.

Colonel Fisher, who sat in on the broadcast shook his head and joked about the Antoric high command.

"This reminds me so much of that idiot who was in charge in Baghdad. If brains were made of dynamite, that silly son of a bitch couldn't blow his nose."

The commanders all agreed it did not look too promising for peace. The ground offensive was ominously looming on the not so distant horizon.

Fisher invited Yates and Edwards back to his quarters for a short meeting. LCDR Hall was put in charge as they left the bridge. The three men sat down in Fisher's compartment. He opened a cabinet and took out a flask, some ice, and three leafy sprigs. He poured the liquid into glasses and handed them to his two friends.

"Boys, although your Jamison's is a fine delectable tribute to anyone's palate, a man just has to change his choice in taste once in awhile. Feast yourselves on these genuine synthetic mint juleps. This is the drink of choice of many a fine southern gentleman in the south. Down the hatch," Fisher toasted.

"Down the hatch," was echoed by Yates and Edwards.

The men finished their drinks and Captain Yates asked,

"Sam, what's on your mind? You called us here for a reason, didn't you?"

"No, I just like to share a drink with friends before I go into battle. By the way, you need to promote your Ensign Washington. I gave him my recipe for this concoction and I think he did a damn good job on it," Fisher replied.

"I agree, this is a fine beverage. I could drink these all day long. We may have to share this find with our friends on the ORION," Edwards stated.

The friends deliberated over the current state of affairs for a while. They prepared to head up to the officer's mess, when a sudden clamor blared out from the ships P.A. system. GONG, GONG, WHOOP, WHOOP, WHOOP, -- "BATTLE STATIONS, BATTLE STATIONS, ALL HANDS MAN YOUR BATTLE STATIONS".

Yates, Edwards and Fisher rushed to the bridge in response to the newest alarm. They arrived to find LCDR Hall concentrating on the screen. He advised that a suspicious lone ship was approaching at a non-threatening speed.

"I wonder what the hell they're up to?" Yates thought out loud. "Randy, launch a probe with a war head on it and detonate about three thousand yards off their bow," the captain ordered.

LCDR Hall shot the probe out of Connie's port torpedo tube and it detonated near the target, as planned. No response came from the inbound ship and it remained on a direct course towards the two star cruisers.

"Captain, I have Captain Meyers standing by on the radio," Lieutenant Lister called out.

"Ken, what can I do for you?" Yates transmitted.

"I don't like the feel of this Al, it may be a trick," Meyers warned.

"I'm thinking the same thing myself. I'll give it a little more time, if nothing happens I'll blast it before it gets too close to the ships. Lister is trying to hail the vessel now," Yates finished.

Lister had no response from her attempts to contact the alien vessel. Nothing but dead silence emitted from the alien ship.

"LCDR Hall, launch two air to air missiles, I don't want them any closer," Yates ordered.

The missiles were launched and made their way to the enemy ship and exploded. A gigantic red and yellow ball of fire erupted and rocked the CONSTELLATION and ORION.

"What the hell was in that thing?" Edwards nervously asked.

"I don't know, but it wasn't leprechauns. The bastards tried to trick us with a bomb," Yates replied.

"Ralf, advise ORION and LCDR Lewis to get ready. It's time to show these pukes we mean business. Have them start hitting the secondary targets as per the plan," Yates ordered.

Commander Edwards alerted the ORION and the CONSTELLATION'S air groups, and the bombing sorties were soon underway. LCDR Hall and LCDR Mead reported back to their ships of heavy anti air craft fire. The resistance was immense, but far from accurate. The F-56-A and ASC-1 fighters had no trouble weaving in and out of the enemy air defense measures and struck their targets precisely. The deception of the actual target went on for two days, and on the third night the bombing effort intensified, drawing enemy troop concentration to the hoax targets. Communication and radar facilities were among the high priority objectives. Most of them were knocked out of action, giving the two star cruisers the stealth they needed to sneak into the landing zone five miles south of the capitol city, Zabia.

The CONSTELLATION touched down, followed close by the ORION. They stayed on the ground long enough to offload the tanks and fighting vehicles of the army detachments from the ships. Colonel Fisher and Mead would drive to the outskirts of the city in two columns, then fan out for the attack. The darkness of the night sky would help conceal their movement and catch the enemy off guard and by complete surprise.

The star cruisers took off and headed back into space to await the word of the main assault. About three o'clock in the morning, still under the cover of darkness the armored columns started to fan out, ready for the attack. The go signal was passed along to the fighter craft attacking the secondary targets to now divert their attention to the prime objective. LCDR's Lewis and Mead turned their birds of prey north to attack Zabia. Within minutes the tank crews on the ground heard the thunderous roar of the war birds. Fisher fired a red flare into the sky; it was the signal for the ground troops to start their offensive. The tanks started to fire their big guns and machine guns, as the fighter craft started bombing and staffing runs on the city. The entire area was one constant roar of thunder as explosions replaced the quiet of night, and the dark sky was lit up with illuminations from the explosions. CONSTELLATION and ORION entered the battle, plummeting the city with their vast array of lasers and missiles. The city was in complete chaos as the battle progressed inward.

"CONSTELLATION, CONSTELLATION, this is Fisher. Over. We need some air support on our rear flank. Those little green critters are massing up to attack. I don't want to be caught in the middle between the top of the tree and the ground like a treed coon," he called.

"Colonel, we roger, we have fighters on the way to take them out," Lister transmitted back.

A group of Golden Hawks commanded by LCDR Jack Mead drew down on the massing Antoric counter offensive and left the ground scorched and soiled, littered with bloodied green bodies. As his command turned to rejoin the main battle, he picked up a formation of Antoric fighters coming in fast.

"All right men, let's drop those birds before they do anyone harm," he called to his pilots.

Mead and his men engaged the approaching green ships in an impressive dog fight. The first wave was taken out of action and a second wave snuck up. The second group was a bit more skilled in aerial combat than the first and proved to be a challenge. The fighters swerved at each other and climbed and turned, trying to avoid being the next casualty. All the while the sky was lit up with laser and gun fire, looking like fire works on the fourth of July. Mead had two of the enemy ships on his tail, he couldn't seem to shake them off and he called for help.

"Mike, give me a hand over here, these bastards are all over me," Mead called.

His wing man came in to help, as did a second fighter - as they closed in, the unthinkable happened. Both enemy ships opened up with every gun they had and Mead's F-56-A blew up, falling to the ground burning brightly in the darkness.

The two fighter pilots, now overcome with rage, attacked their commander's assailants and ruthlessly destroyed them as they tried to retreat to safety. Mead's fighter group flew over and searched the wreckage of their commander to see if he was alive. As they passed over it they saw his smoldering body in the cockpit, his hands still on the controls. The news of this loss was radioed back to the ORION and Captain Meyers lowered his head in silent prayer. Jack and he had been good friends.

The battle was now well into the afternoon hours. The Antorics put up a harder fought ground battle than they did in the air or in space. Casualties were being shuttled up to star cruisers for treatment of their wounds. The sick bays were once again in full operation, with staff struggling to save the lives of their comrades injured in conflict. Both Fisher and Reed were starting to run low on ammo. The shuttles, when returning from ambulance duty, doubled as supply ships on the return flights. They could not keep up with the constant demand for ordinance needed by the army fighting on the ground. Yates, well aware of the shortages, held a meeting with Captain Meyers by electronic means.

"Ken, please accept my condolences for LCDR Mead. He was a good man," Yates sympathized.

"Thanks Al, the two of us raised a lot of hell together," Meyers replied.

"Things could start going sour on the ground real soon, we have a supply problem. I have about eight nukes left. I think the sooner we bring this mess to a close the better off we will be," Yates rationalized.

"I have twelve left on board. We caught them by surprise, but now they are starting to re-group in about six locations. If those forces reach the main operational area the army will be pressed pretty hard, like the Nazi Army at Leningrad. We can't let that happen, Al," Meyers replied.

"I spoke with Sam earlier, he is in agreement. He wants the two largest formations toasted first. If those bastards have any inkling of intelligence, this may persuade them to give up. Otherwise we are in deep shit; we have underestimated their resolve," Yates admitted.

The decision to use nuclear weapons on the surface was agreed to. The coordinates for the missiles were fed into the fire control consoles on both ships and all units on the ground were notified of the incoming persuaders. The missiles hit their targets, completely obliterating the massing Antoric forces. The war continued on. The earth commanders concluded it would take another deadly display to convince the enemy to stop fighting. This time four targets were selected, and once again the nuclear persuaders dealt out their message of doom, destroying the remaining enemy concentrations.

Fisher and Reed's forces had made it into the center of the city; the entire metropolis was littered with the bodies of Antoric military and civilian casualties. The heat from burning structures added to the decomposition of the corpses, spreading the stench of death everywhere. The fighting was fierce, and in many instances resulted in to hand to hand combat. Supplies were running low on both sides as the two warring opponents resorted to any means possible to destroy the other. Fisher was calling up the last of his supplies and stopped in the middle of his radio transmission. Antoric units were throwing their weapons down and walking out into the open. Fisher ordered his men to cease fire and called up to CONSTELLATION.

"This is Fisher, patch me to Captain Yates," he yelled into his radio.

"This is Yates, go ahead colonel," Yates replied.

"The green bastards are starting to surrender. I think the battle is drawing to a close," Fisher conveyed.

"ORION is getting in some reports now. Lister just handed them to me. Maybe the nukes did their thing and knocked some sense into these guys," Yates radioed.

The fighting slowly drew to a halt and a message came from the Antoric leaders, they wanted to meet and bring to a close the war between the two peoples.

Two delegates from the Antoric government were shuttled to CONSTELLATION for a summit to end hostilities. Hasen, the ruler and Metrad were escorted to the deck 6 conference room to meet with Yates, Edwards and Fisher from CONSTELLATION and Meyers, Page and Reed from the ORION. Yates opened the meeting with a question.

"Why did you attack us? We did nothing to provoke the bloodshed and untold loss of lives? We tried to communicate with you and your response was one of trickery and violence."

Hasen, with the help of the translator unit answered the captain's question. "We are an old people, we learned long ago not to trust others from races not of our own. Many of your centuries ago we were explorers of space like yourselves and we found nothing but danger and treachery from beings of other worlds."

"You can't judge other races from the misdeeds of a few. We travel in peace and had no intentions of even making contact with your world," Edwards remarked.

"The very least you could have done was to talk with us. What gives you the right to arbitrarily attack any ship in space for no reason at all? As Captain Yates stated, it would have prevented the unnecessary loss of innocent lives," Meyers added.

Metrad spoke of mistrust. "Hasen has made reference to the mistrust of others. This part of space is inhabited by factions of thieves and murderers. We have trusted some and have been tricked. It is our law not to let others inside our sphere of influence. We have to protect our people."

"Kind of reminds you of Zelcore or the Mid-East, doesn't it? No one trusts anyone and the whole place is a big shooting gallery, shoot first and ask questions later if there is anyone left alive" Fisher commented.

"It's all right to challenge a strange ship entering your backyard to learn of their intentions, but it's another to blatantly wage war against them on the assumption they are hostile. We all have the right to defend ourselves when faced with the threat of danger. Ask first, then shoot. Take a good look at your world the destruction and the loss of thousands of lives. This whole catastrophe could have been avoided," Yates added.

After six hours of negotiations, the meeting concluded with a truce being signed. The Antorics declined any help in rebuilding the destroyed cities, they just wished for the earthlings to leave their planet system.

Yates assured the two ships from earth would leave as soon as the army elements were brought back on board. He also added that they may pass through the Antoric system in the future and expected a guarantee of safe passage which was agreed to in the terms of the truce.

CONSTELLATION and ORION once again touched down on the planet's surface to retrieve the tired army troops. A full combat patrol of fighters flew above to provide a CAP while the tanks and men were loaded up. The last of the iron war horses rolled up the ramp into the hanger decks, then to an elevator in the aft end of the bay to be secured in the holding compartments down below. The hanger doors were slid shut on both ships and they took off back to the cosmos. The ships traveled towards the outer planets of the system and came to a halt. Yates and Edwards took a shuttle craft to the ORION for a meeting to determine a course of action. The meeting took place in the air operations debriefing room.

"Welcome aboard ORION, gentlemen. Make yourselves at home" Meyers greeted, as he opened the meeting.

"ORION is in need of repair. I don't think we will survive well if we meet some other of your friends in battle. The problem is, for the majority of the repairs we need to be at a base, they can't be done in space. Do you know of a nearby AMACO station?" Meyers asked.

"The next closest friendly system is Zelcor, but I don't know if they would be of much help" Edwards suggested.

"Oh, those must be the folks you made friendly by force," Page joked.

"It took some arm bending, but they bent our way," Yates shot back. He then continued, "I suggest we make a run to Flox. Hell, not only can they repair this ship, but they can upgrade it to be almost as efficient as CONSTELLATION," Yates boasted.

After a few more digs of friendly ship rivalry, the two cruisers set course for the safe waters of the Flox system. Due to engine damage and ORION not being as technically advanced as Connie, it was anticipated the trip would be a lengthy one. Hopefully the trip would be uneventful, as the crews of both ships were tired and worn and well-deserving of a friendly port of call.

CHAPTER 9

# THE YARDS, REST, HELP AND DANGER

The two sister ships departed the Antoric system and were on a course that would take them to Flox for repairs. As they were half way between the Antoric and Zelcor planetary systems, crews on both ships were once again decked out in dress uniforms to pay their final tributes to fallen comrades. The Washington brothers hooked up a ship to ship audio/video connection for the duel service. Father Daniel O'Rourke led the service prayer.

"Friends we are gathered here today to say farewell to our shipmates who have fallen in battle. Their efforts were gallant as they struggled to save their fellow crew and ships. We know of the hereafter - this is now their final resting place. The evils of war do have its good aspects, for it will bring out the goodness of the good and their reward will be a just one in heaven, we ask of You to let these brave men's souls to enter into Your kingdom."

Father Delaney then started with his sermon.

"Once again we are gathered here in this time of sorrow to pay tribute to the loss of our friends who have given their lives in battle. Not only for those of CONSTELLATION, but for those from ORION as well. We have been here many times in our travels and now we are joined in sorrow by our fellow service men and women from our sister ship. We were not asked to join in this conflict, it was forced upon us. I thank the Lord for the wisdom he has bestowed on our commanders, for without His help the consequences could have been far much worse. Let us bow our heads in prayer. Oh, Lord we thank Thee for the privilege of sharing our lives with the departed. Just by the knowing of them, our lives have been richly blessed. We feel comfort in knowing their souls now rest with You in Your hands as they enter Your house to spend eternity in heaven."

The crews on both ships moved up to the observation decks as the sound of Amazing Grace echoed through the corridors. As the hanger bay doors slid open the deceased were passed through to the voids of outer space, their final resting place. Commanding officers and clergy were on hand to help consol those overwhelmed with grief and to honor the memory of the dead.

Yates and Meyers held an electronic conference to decide how the air operations department would work together. ORION was left without a flight officer when LCDR Jack Mead was killed in battle on Antoric-9

"Al, most of the pilots on board here don't have the experience to command an entire wing, hell most of them are rookies. I don't know if you have someone in mind that we could transfer over here or not," Meyers stated.

"I have discussed this idea with Doug Lewis and I would like to run it by you to see what you think about it. We could have Doug take command of both groups. Your flight X.O. could manage the day to day operations, but if we go back into combat Doug would have complete command. With your approval we would promote him to the rank of commander," Yates explained.

"I don't have a problem with that at all. I think it would enhance the ability of both air groups operating as one instead of separate. I say let's do it," Meyers replied.

"I'll tell him as soon as we get off the air and have him come over to chat with you and to meet the boys," Yates finished.

The two ships were now passing through the Zelcor system and the ZILOD was patrolling the sector of entry and she contacted CONSTELLATION. Yates explained the circumstances of their return voyage to Yalt. The two earth ships were invited to lay over on Zelcor, but Yates advised it was questionable if ORION would be able to take off from the planet to finish the journey to Flox due to the failing of some of her engines. Yalt did agree it may not be good to land on his home planet. Although his world had made remarkable progress with its rebuilding projects, it was doubtful they could be of any assistance in making the needed repairs to the ORION.

As the days passed by, so did the Zelcor system and the sister ships were once again in open space. There was a constant shuttling of technicians between the two ships trying to keep the ORION'S engines operational, but the effort was starting to fail. ORION was down to seven of her engines and she was having a hard time trying to keep up with CONSTELLATION. Both captains prayed they would not have to engage in combat while the ships were in this state of disrepair. Their prayers were answered as the outer planets of the Flox system came into view, and a sigh of relief was breathed at the sight. As they neared the planet of Flox-2 Captain Yates hailed the Tactical Command Center.

"Flox Tactical Command, this is the USS CONSTELLATION. Over."

"CONSTELLATION, welcome back to our home. How may we help you?" a friendly voice asked.

Yates explained what they had been through and how they had run across another ship from earth. He asked permission for both vessels to land and hold over for repairs. The Flox Tactical Command Center once again welcomed their earth friends and granted permission to land at the base outside of Fleddes. The communications center would notify Kalgor to have him meet them at the base. CONSTELLATION touched down first, just in the nick of time as another one of her engines went off line. ORION was offloading her fighters to lighten the load on the ship, lessening the strain on her engines. After the fighters had landed, ORION would attempt to make hers.

ORION started down into the atmosphere and the ship had difficulty maintaining steering control, the strain of entering the atmosphere caused her engines to overheat. She was down to five engines, and two of them were in marginal shape. The ship bounced and veered back and forth on her approach and she came in hard. The massive ship bounced several times on the hard surface and then snuggled the runway, coming to rest behind CONSTELLATION.

The ramps of both ships were lowered and the two captains walked out onto the tarmac to greet Kalgor, who was waiting for them.

"Alex, my good friend, it is good to see you again. I understand your travels have not been pleasant. You are always welcome to rest here and have your space craft repaired," greeted Kalgor.

"Thank you Kalgor. The hospitality of your people holds a warm place in our hearts. Let me introduce to you Captain Ken Meyers, the commander of the USS ORION. If not for him and his ship, we would not be talking with each other today," Yates replied.

After introductions, Kalgor was invited aboard CONSTELLATION where the command staff of ORION had assembled. He shook hands with his old friends and now some new friends and welcomed each one as he met them. A three day liberty was granted to both crews as the Flox technicians inspected the star cruisers for the needed repairs and upgrades to the ships. Before the crew was dismissed, Kalgor got Yates aside and told him of some very important news.

"Alex, I know you are in need of rest. Tomorrow we must meet, we may have found a way for you and your people to return to your home," informed Kalgor.

Yates beamed with a smile of relief and questioned his friend.

"How? Where? It would be a blessing. We have been through a lot and have feared we may be destined to live out the rest of our lives in a constant hostile environment, never to see our families again. Please tell me now."

"My friend, take today and rest. I have duties I must perform today. We will meet tomorrow over a nice cool drink of Long Island Lemoc. My taste buds have been yearning for its flavor for quite some time," Kalgor insisted.

That evening Yates met with Fisher, Edwards and Meyers over drinks in his quarters. He informed them of the news Kalgor had imparted and that perhaps their search would soon be over.

"My, that is certainly good news Al, I'm elated with the possibility of going home. I can't tell you how I feel. We have experienced a lot on this mission and the good outweighs the bad, but the bad is a heavier burden to carry," Edwards philosophized.

"It's been a hard trip, boys. We lost a lot of good men. But we have also done a lot of good. And that my friends is something we all can be proud of," Fisher added.

"My crew has only been on this journey for a very short time, and by God I think we have had our fill. I think we have enough stories to tell our grandchildren's children. I'm glad we were able to find each other. Hell, the odds of us running into each other must be astronomical," Meyers spoke.

"It's not over yet, we will find out the hows and whys tomorrow. It is a weight off my shoulders just to know we may be finally going home, I miss my wife and family immensely. I will be most grateful to turn command over to some one else; I need a rest," Yates conveyed.

The beverages were finished and Yates invited the men to his meeting with Kalgor set for the following morning as they left his quarters to retire for the night.

The morning broke and Kalgor, as promised, arrived at CONSTELLATION. Yates met him at the hanger deck and escorted him to the bridge conference room. The other officers were in attendance.

"Kalgor, I was up most of the night in anticipation of the news you have for us. Please enlighten us, we have grown weary of battle and travel and the hopes of returning to our home planet is of the most importance," Yates excitedly insisted.

"Our science ministry was confused and misinformed you on how to find your 'worm hole'. We are friends with the people of Vantec, and this race has mastered the use of these 'worm holes' for their own space travel. The hole does move as we have said, but only in a relatively small area. The same hole appears and disappears according to cosmic forces in any given system. We have also learned that these holes are connected at certain times and a ship could virtually travel the entire spectrum of space," Kalgor explained.

"Wow, these phenomena are a lot to think about. It's hard to grasp its concept," Yates thought out loud.

"How do you know which and what holes to connect to when you find them?" Meyers asked.

"I have explained your plight to the Vantec people. They are mapping out for you your voyage. I was going to send ships out to find you, but, as fate has it, you returned," Kalgor replied.

"How about that, an interstate system in space! I hope the toll roads are cheap. We have paid a high toll so far," Edwards injected.

"The Vantec system is on the far side of ours. You will have to travel through hostile space into the Bedzal system. I wish you luck as you pass through there, they wish to seek vengeance on the people of earth," Kalgor warned.

"Well isn't that just Jim Dandy. We get to kick those Bedzal sons of bitches all over again! "Fisher exclaimed.

"Their battle fleet should still be down from the last time we partied with them. Who knows, they may have learned their lesson and will think twice before they want to pick a fight with us again and now they have two earth ships to deal with," Yates expounded.

The meeting lasted for an hour longer and basically consisted of questions and answers. At the end, Yates grinned and once again reached under the table and pulled out a pitcher of the sparkling amber liquid. Kalgor smiled as the captain poured drinks for everyone. With the majority of the crew on leave, the happy hour turned into several as the friends celebrated the hopeful news and rekindled friendships.

As the crew drifted back from liberty, repair work and upgrades to both ships got underway. The Flox technicians would bring ORION to the same level of advancement as CONSTELLATION was. Crews from both ships were given training on how to use the new equipment installed. The training would soon be put to use when the ships returned to space for their journey home.

The day of departure from Flox came upon them and the two earth star cruisers prepared to leave their safe haven once again. Kalgor, who came to see his friends off, bid farewell to them and wished them all a safe journey. As Yates and Kalgor shook hands, the captain spoke to him.

"We shall meet again. I trust one day you will visit my world. Take care my friend."

Kalgor stepped down from the ship and the hanger bay door slid shut. The sister ships slowly turned and positioned themselves on the runway for take off. The roar of the engines from both ships echoed across the base as they taxied down the runway and faded into the bright sky as the star cruisers lifted their way back into space.

The earth ships would chart new ground as they headed to the far side of the Flox system into hostile territory. The crews and their ships were well prepared for the Bedzals, as they expected their presence would be less than welcome.

With the Flox system now just a twinkle of the vast star fields, CONSTELLATION and ORION were on a high state of alert as they drew closer to the unfriendly star system of their former foe. Commander Lewis sent constant fighter patrols out in front of the two ships for early detection of hostile craft.

As the earthlings drew closer to the planet of Bedzal-4, they slowed their speed. With the four moons of this planet and an asteroid belt flowing through it, it would be a prime area to ambush any passers-by using the concealment supplied by nature. The two star vessels were now cruising side by side, ORION to CONSTELLATION'S port side.

"Captain Meyers, I'm not quite sure how to use the new scanners installed on the ship. It's hard to distinguish clutter from a target; however, this blip over here seems to be giving off a little different echo return," Ensign Keen reported.

Meyers and LCDR Adams went over to the consol to see if they could help decipher the target.

"It does appear to be giving off a little different echo captain. I'm going to contact CONSTELLATION to get their opinion on it," Adams advised.

"Wait sir, maybe it is clutter from the belt. Look, there are a lot more readings now," Keen countered.

Just as Ensign Keen finished his statement, WHOMP, WHOMP, WHOMP, WHOMP was heard and the ORION shook. The ship had just been hit by four Bedzal torpedoes and the radar screen came alive with hundreds of incoming blips representing enemy ships.

"Commander Page, bring ORION to battle stations and notify CONSTELLATION we are under attack," Captain Meyers ordered.

GONG, GONG, GONG, WHOOP, WHOOP, WHOOP "BATTLE STATIONS, BATTLE STATIONS, ALL HANDS MAN YOUR BATTLE STATIONS. THIS IS NOT A DRILL" echoed throughout the ship.

Commander Page established a communications link with CONSTELLATION and informed her executive officer of the attack.

"Ralf, we have been hit. We also show multiple targets coming at us from the port side and off our bow. We are engaging," Page reported.

"Chris, we see them, Connie is at battle stations and we have targets coming at us from starboard. Lewis has already called for all fighters to deploy and attack. How bad is ORION hurt?" Edwards replied.

"Damage control hasn't reported back yet, but it felt bad. We have light smoke spreading throughout the ship. I'll get back to you, it's starting to get a little hectic in here," Page finished.

The guns on both ships were firing at full capacity, as well as the laser cannons and torpedoes, all announcing the wrath of the earth ships. Commander Lewis divided his fighters into four units. A combat air patrol would provide protection to the sister star cruisers, one unit each would attack enemy ships coming in from the port and starboard and the last unit would attack the inbounds coming directly at the ships from the front.

It appeared the Bedzals had had enough time to rearm their military - the force was considerately larger than it was at the end of the Flox / Bedzal conflict some months earlier. The force was determined to destroy the earth ships in this most elaborate ambush.

The Bedzals were now bringing in larger, more powerful war ships, surrounding CONSTELLATION and ORION. Commander Lewis and his fighters were being pushed back from all directions. The Bedzals were enjoying their sweet revenge from the punishment CONSTELLAION inflicted on them the last time they had met in battle.

ORION was hit hard several more times. LCDR Bert Adams was blown off the ship while he was making repairs to the fire control relay on one of the lower port side gun turrets. Meyers called CONSTELLATION and advised Yates he had lost his weapons officer and asked if there was anyone onboard who could replace him until the battle ended. LCDR Hall spoke confidently of Washington's ability to maintain Connie's integrity to fight and volunteered to help out on the ORION.

"Tyrone, we are counting on you to keep our asses from getting blown up. You're in charge of ships defenses while LCDR Hall is away. If you don't think you can handle it, let me know now," Yates questioned.

"Don't worry skipper, I'll blow them muthas all the way back to the big dipper, if that would make you chipper? And I'll kick them in the zipper for the old gippa," Washington rhymed back.

"I'll take that as a yes," Yates replied.

The battle heated up and the two star cruisers started to take more punishment from the Bedzal onslaught. ORION had radioed CONSTELLATION that she was now fighting the battle blind. Her radar and scanner systems had been knocked out. She would have to rely on the eyes of her sister ship and fighter craft for targeting the incoming ships and missiles.

Commander Edwards was assisting Ensign Washington at the weapons consol. The ensign had more than he could handle. The asteroid belt did its part to confuse targeting enemy ships with its clutter.

"Hey, X.O. look at this bunch of dots up here in the corner. Looks like them yellow crackers are wanting to try to kick our ass from the starboard bow, don't it?" Washington asked.

"I think you're right Tyrone. The captain needs to know this now," Edwards advised.

"Yo Alex, my man. We gots a bunch of yellow submarines off the starboard bow. I think we should nuke the fuckers," Washington shouted.

Yates went down to his station and saw for himself, there were over six hundred ships massing for a run at the navy space elements.

"Mr. Washington, I believe you are more than correct on your reading of the intelligence. Punch in the coordinates of the enemy ship concentration and relay it over to ORION. Let's blast those Bedzal bastards out of the sky before they have a chance to make a run at us. Also, when these matters at hand are over with, we need to sit down and have a little father and son chat about military protocol," Yates ordered.

The target information was passed on to the ORION and within minutes both ships launched their nuclear missiles at the huge target Washington saw on his screen. The eight deadly guided projectiles made radio active rubbish on the Bedzal fleet.

"They still haven't learned, have they? They still keep grouping together in plain view before they are anywhere close to being ready for an assault," Edwards laughed.

Several more large concentrations of Bedzal ships were spotted by radar and they met the same fate as the previous one. The tide of battle was starting to change in favor of the earth travelers as the Bedzal forces changed gears from offence to defense. Four enemy fighters snuck in from behind the star cruisers and smashed into the stern of ORION, causing heavy damage. Fire and smoke drifted off from her burning hull into space. She was not quite done for yet and continued to fire her weapons that were still intact.

"CONSTELLATION, CONSTELLATION, this is ORION. Over." LTJG Lister notified Yates she had an urgent call from Captain Meyers. She patched over to the radar consol where he was standing.

"Go ahead Ken, what do you need?" Yates asked.

"Al, ORION is in bad shape, we can't take too much more. My engineering department is a shambles, we only have five engines on line. All the sick bay areas are inundated with casualties and the medical staff can't keep up. If we can find a safe haven we need to evacuate them over to Connie. I only have about forty five percent weapons capability, and to top things off the outer hull has been breached in three locations. We are just about dead in the water," Meyers replied.

"Ken, are your nukes still intact?" Yates asked.

"Stand by, I'll find out. -------- Al, yes they are."

"O.K., we see one big group massing to make a run at us. They are about fifty thousand yards off your port bow. We are sending the targeting info over to you now. Launch four nukes, we will do the same. Then change your course 0-9-0 degrees right to a new heading of 0-6-0 and scoot out at your best speed. Lewis is putting together a CAP for you. We will cover your withdrawal and catch up with you later. I think if we take out this last pocket of them, they will cut off the attack and let us go," Yates instructed.

"I hope you're right Al, It's questionable if we will be able to make it home," Meyers radioed.

"Don't worry Ken, we will all make it," Yates concluded.

Yates' hunch was right, as the last foray of nukes hit their target, the balance of the Bedzal fleet started to fall back. Commander Lewis took care of a few stragglers that had a death wish. ORION vacated the battle zone and was now able to commit what was left of her crew to perform damage control and to try and shore up the ship.

CONSTELLATION and the fighters left the area together and headed to rendezvous with her sister.

CONSTELLATION followed a trail of debris from ORION and caught up with her. As they got into visual range they saw large plumes of smoke and fire belching out into space as explosions spewed additional fragments of the ship in her wake.

"Lieutenant Lister, patch me through to ORION," Yates ordered.

"Ken, what is your status? Your ship doesn't look good from here," Yates asked.

"It's bad, Al. Lewis has already begun to evacuate the wounded over to your ship using the transports. We have fires throughout sixty percent of the ship. Life support is failing and we're running on three main engines and auxiliaries. As soon as the wounded are out of here I'm going to start sending my crew over. Al, ORION is dying," Meyers replied.

"Ralf, contact Fisher and see if he can have some of his men help offload the wounded from the transports and bring them to sick bay. ORION doesn't have much time. The faster we move here, the more souls may be saved," Yates ordered.

Commander Edwards, Colonel Fisher and his men rushed to the hanger deck and assisted with the moving of the wounded ORION crew. LCDR Hall came back with one of the shuttles and advised Yates there was no hope of saving the ORION. Some of the engineering staff were already starting to suffer the effects of radiation as it leaked from ORIONS reactors.

The injured had all been evacuated and now the crew was being shuttled over to CONSTELLATION on transports from both ships. The offloading of the wounded was a slow process. As the transports landed inside the hanger deck or departed, the ships had to wait as the hanger deck pressurized or depressurized. Valuable time was lost due to this process.

Captain Meyers knew his ship had no hope of survival. He and the command staff were trying to hold ORION together for as long as they could so that they could get as many of the crew off as possible. Meyers called down to the engineering department to ascertain how much longer he could expect power for the ship. He tried to reach LCDR Finch by radio several times, but he had no answer. Meyers looked over to his X.O. and said in a panicky voice, " Chris

I can't reach Mike, see if you can make it down to engineering and find out how much longer we have."

Commander Page nodded his head and exited the bridge. Page ran to the elevator, but it was out of order, he rushed down the smoke filled corridor to the next set, but they also were not working. He then managed to find his way down to a stairway and started his decent down several decks. Fighting his way through smoke and fire he managed to reach the main engineering center. As he pushed wreckage out of his way to gain entry he gazed through the smoke at dead crewmen littering the deck. He found LCDR Finch who was badly burned leaning over one of the engine consoles still trying to keep one of the mains operating.

"Mike, Mike, how bad are we, how long do we have?" Page asked in a feverous voice.

Finch, who was suffering from exhaustion, radiation burns, and coughing from the smoke looked at him with a dazed expression and replied, "Chris, there is no hope, we are finished. Get the hell out of here while you can. These things are going to blow any minute now. Everything is breached I can't contain the radiation, save yourself."

Commander Page rushed over to him as to help him out of the compartment, LCDR Finch raised his hand to stop him and said, "Chris, I'm already dead get out, I've been exposed to too much of this shit, get out, seal the hatch behind you."

Page headed to the advice of his shipmate and slowly turned to exit the compartment as he reached the hatch he turned to look at his friend to wish him luck, and saw his friend slowly slither to the deck gasping for his last breath.

Page knew to well that this may be the fate of everyone on board and prayed for time to evacuate as many of the crew as possible from this terrible ordeal, and actually hoped that the ship would blow up for those who could not be rescued so that they would not have to suffer as his friend LCDR Finch did.

The commander fought his way back to the bridge. Several more explosions rocked the star cruiser blocking passage ways. Page made it back to his captain to give his report to Meyers, as he entered Meyers turned to see who it was. Page just glared at the captain with a look of despair on his face. The captain did not have to ask him how bad things were.

"Chris get aboard one of the shuttles now. No use in the two of us going down with ORION, that's an order." Meyers stated in desperation.

"With all due respect sir, I'll stay with you on the bridge. Anyone forward "C" section aint going anywhere." Page replied.

"I suppose I better tell Alex we won't be playing cards tonight. It's been a privilege serving with you. Let's do what we can." Meyers countered

"Captain Yates, I have Captain Meyers standing by on the radio," Lister advised.

"What is it Ken?" Yates asked.

"Al, you better back Connie off. Stop the transports, we're loosing the ship," Meyers stated.

"Ken, get the hell out of there!" Yates exclaimed.

"I have two transports left on board, we have people trapped. We're going to try and get to them before we blow. How many of my people do you have?" Meyers asked.

"Including the wounded, only about four hundred," Yates answered.

"Shit, I still have thirty one hundred left on board. Al, we haven't

– hold on a second. Al, Get your ship away now, the reactors are blowing. Move it Al!!"

Meyers yelled.

Yates ordered the helm to full reverse and to back away, veering to the right. The bridge crew had their eyes glued to the main viewing screen and watched as the ORION slowly drifted to a stop. The once mighty star cruiser had been reduced to a burning hulk dead in space. The helpless crew of CONSTELLATION stood by as the last transport from ORION cleared the hanger bay door in a desperate flee to safety. The ORION blew apart in a bright red and orange blaze of fire. ORION, with thirty one hundred of her crew, perished in the massive explosion.

Yates stood on the bridge, devastated as he watched the last embers of his friend's ship dwindle into the darkness of space. Yates put his hand over his eyes as to cover his emotions he then collapsed onto the deck from mental pain and anguish. Commander Edwards and LCDR Hall helped him up and assisted him to his quarters.

"Ralf, I need a little rest, you're in command for a while," the captain said softly as he closed his eyes. As Commander Edwards was closing the door he heard the captain whimper blaming himself for the loss of ORION.

CHAPTER 10

# ASSISTANCE FROM VANTEC AND HOME

CONSTELLATION once again found herself traveling through space alone. Commander Lewis and LT. Marsh were busy reconfiguring Connie's lower holds to house the additional fighters now on board from the ORION. Ensign Washington was scrambling around the ship to find out if his brother Reggie had made it to safety.

Washington found his brother in the main sick bay area of the ship. He was covered with gauze bandages recovering from burns he received when his gun turret caught fire.

"Reggie, shit man you made it. I was scared to death when your ship blew. We're going home now brother. Just you wait and see, when The Washington brothers return, we gonna be hero's. We gonna paint the city red, aint no one gonna separate us again." Washington said while comforting his brother as tears ran down his face.

Father Delaney and LCDR Wang were busy helping Dr. Jagman in sick bay. This was the most injuries his area had to deal with yet caring for wounded of two ships. The majority of the cases were serious.

LCDR Malloy and LT Williams were checking Connie for battle damage and assigning crews to complete the repairs where needed.

Commander Edwards, LCDR Hall and Colonel Fisher were charting a course for the Vantec system and maintaining a vigilant sweep of space for any hostile Bedzal ships still wanting to fight.

Captain Yates was still hold up in his quarters, not wanting to see anyone. He was trying to deal with the loss of the ORION's crew. He still blamed himself for their demise.

The mood aboard CONSTELLATION was dismal, at best. The entire crew was suffering from shock and disbelief over the destruction of their sister ship and the loss of her crew, who so many had befriended.

The last of the casualties had been treated in sick bay and the staff was near exhaustion. Jagman, Wang and Delaney went to the officer's mess for coffee and a much needed break.

"I'm beat. My God it's been over seventy two hours since we started. My feet are killing me," Jagman stated as he clutched his coffee cup between his two hands.

"Yes, it was a rough session. Those army medics certainly pulled their own weight. I'm amazed at how resourceful they are. Has anyone heard from the captain? Is he still locked in his quarters? Wang asked.

Father Delaney replied, "Yes, I spoke with Commander Edwards earlier, he hasn't seen anyone. Nor has he eaten. I'm going to stop by and try to talk with him. He is blaming himself for the destruction of

ORION. He feels he should have ordered her out of the area sooner than what he did. Captain Meyers had the final say of what his ship was to do. He opted to fight for as long as his ship could. These two captains must have been cut from the same tree."

"Father, that is nonsense. He couldn't do anything for the ship. It was out of his control. Captain Meyers knew of his options if the shoe was on the other foot Captain Yates would have done the same thing," Wang replied.

"I know, we all are aware of how the captain feels about his responsibilities to the crew. He was the most experienced officer and felt he needed to do more. His compassion for others just may be his undoing. I'm going to see him now. He must be torturing himself with unjustified guilt," Delaney finished.

Delaney left his friends and proceeded to the captain's quarters. He knocked on his door, no response. He knocked a second time and got an answer.

"I asked not to be disturbed, who is it?" Yates shouted.

"Captain, it is Father Delaney. I wish to talk with you. I am not leaving until I do so," Delaney insisted.

"Very well." The door was unlocked.

The Father was shocked at the sight of his captain. Yates was unshaven, with unkempt hair, wearing a wrinkled unbuttoned uniform. His face was pale and drawn from sorrow and pain.

"What is it Father? Can't you see I want to be left alone?" Yates harshly asked.

"I know my son. I am not going to let you kill yourself spiritually. Captain Meyers would not approve of your self-imposed exile. He would also not approve of you blaming yourself of the fate of ORION," Delaney insisted gently.

"You're wrong Father, I was the senior commander. I should have ordered him out when he first advised he was in trouble. I waited too long and they're dead. The whole crew is dead" Yates scolded.

"Alex, he was the captain of his ship, the same as you. He knew of his responsibility. You know damn good and well he would not have left CONSTELLATION to fend for herself. He waited until he could no longer fight. It was his decision. Don't blame yourself. The blame is not yours," Delaney consoled.

"Father, over three thousand lives were lost, how could I have helped to save them?" Yates asked as he fell to his knees weeping.

The priest knelt down and prayed aloud for strength for the captain to overcome his guilt. Delaney held him for a short time and then said to him softly and firmly,

"Captain your crew is keeping CONSTELLATION running. They respect their captain and they need their captain. They need their captain to bring them home. Don't let them down, and for God's sake don't let yourself down. Alex, you have gotten us this far, now take us the rest of the way home."

"Father, thank you. You are right. We must get home. I'm sorry for my actions, I… I just felt sick when ORION blew. I don't know what came over me, it was such a waste, those fine brave men and women," Yates replied.

"I know what came over you, that is why you command the respect you do. Your crew knows you care about each and every one of them. That is the precise reason why they work to keep your ship going. They know you would not steer them wrong," Delaney consoled.

Yates stood quietly for a moment, then looked Father Delaney firmly in the eye. He asked him to prepare a memorial prayer to be read over the P.A. system later that day. The father said he would take care of it and left so the captain could further gather his composure. Yates showered and shaved and changed into a fresh uniform, the first steps of readying himself to retake his command. At first it was hard to proceed; he stopped at his cabin door and asked himself if he was ready. He walked slowly out into the corridor, feeling so alone. He put one foot in front of the other, cautious at first. The captain walked tall and proud. as he gained more self-confidence, quickening his pace with each step.

Yates entered the bridge and watched his crew hard at work. He was proud of them, they were well trained. Commander Edwards glanced up to see who had entered and gave a warm smile when he saw it was the captain. Edwards stood fast and snapped,

"Attention, captain on the bridge!"

The entire bridge crew stood up straight and saluted. Yates himself stood straight and returned their salutes, almost overcome with emotion.

"Commander Edwards, how close are we to the Vantec System?" Yates confidently asked.

"Captain, we are about three days away," Edwards sharply replied.

"Very well. Ship's status?" he asked

"Captain, CONSTELLATION is fully operational. We just have a few minor repairs to complete," Edwards replied.

Yates took the center chair in the bridge and reviewed the log and started to review the status reports. Commander Edwards walked up to him with a cup in his hand that had the ship's crest of the USS ORION S.C.-2 embossed on it and said,

"Al, LCDR Hall is in his quarters trying to get some sleep. He was up for quite a long time. He asked me to give this to you when you came back. It's a farewell gift from Captain Meyers. Al, Ken knew he wasn't going to make it and he wanted you to have this keepsake in remembrance of the ORION."

Yates took the cup and held it in his hands. He had difficulty swallowing. He stared at it for a while, then looked up to his X.O. and said,

"Ralf, let's bring CONSTELLATION and the ORION home. Full speed ahead to Vantec."

Just as the captain gave the order ENS Washington blurted out, "Sheeet, dem  yellow crackers be coming after us. What the fuck is their problem?"

Yates and Edwards rushed to the weapons console and studied the screen. To there surprise a Bedzal battle group consisting of over two hundred ships were closing in on CONSTELLATION. Yates without hesitation gave the order to bring Connie to battle stations.

Washington flipped on the P.A. system announcing, "BATTLE STATIONS, BATTLE STATIONS, GET YO ASSES IN GEAR THE BEDZAL MOTHA FUCKERS ARE ON OUR REAR. THOSE BITCHES ARE GETTING NEAR, BUT HAVE NO FEAR THE CAPTAIN IS HERE."

The ship once again jumped into action as Connie came about to meet her aggressors at the same time Commander Lewis brought his war birds from out of their coop and made runs at the Bedzal forces with fighters from CONSTELLATION and the remnants of ORIONS air wing.

Lewis and his band of warriors picked off the nearest ships of the Bedzal and were ordered back to form a protective barrier in front of Connie. Yates ordered the last of the nuclear missiles be launched to blow a hole in the tight formation of the enemy. The nukes hit there targets punching a hole in the battle group. Lewis was then ordered to pick off the rest of the Bedzal ships at his pleasure.

Yates radioed Lewis and ordered, "Doug don't let any of those bastards stay afloat. If they try to run home knock them out, the spirits of Ken Meyers and the ORION crew are with you."

Lewis replied," Understood sir, I'll make sure one of the ORION's birds has the last kill."

The Bedzals surprised by the resolve of the earthlings started to make a run for it, Lewis and his birds of war would not let them off the hook. One by one the enemy ships were sent to their maker with the last kill being made by an ORION Golden Hawk.

With the radar and scanner screens clear the birds of pray were recalled back to CONSTELLATION. With the achieved victory and no further threat Connie stood down from battle stations and resumed her course to Vantec.

Early evening the crew was asked for a moment of silence as Father Delaney read his memorial prayer over the ship's P.A. system. He also asked for strength for those of ORIONS crew recovering on board CONSTELLATION.

The lone star cruiser drew closer and closer to the Vantec system and her crew started to bounce back from the solemn presence that had overtaken the atmosphere on board. Yates was taking the late watch when LT Marsh came up to him.

"Captain, can I have a moment of your time?"

"Why certainly lieutenant, what is it?" Yates inquired.

"Sir, Ensign King and I want to marry each other while we are still up in space. And we, we were wondering if you would be best man?" Marsh requested.

"John, is she, well you know, is she?" Yates inquisitively asked.

"OHH, NO SIR. She is not," Marsh replied.

"John, thank you. It will be a privilege and an honor, I wish the very best for the both of you," Yates warmly replied.

"Captain, we plan to hold the ceremony after we leave Vantec. Father Delaney said he would perform the nuptials in the ship's chapel," Marsh concluded.

The journey to the Vantec system came to its end as CONSTELLATION entered the small system consisting of two planets. As per Kalgor's instructions, the ship headed to Vantec-1 and circled the planet in a low orbit.

Communications were established with the Vantec council and permission to transport down in a shuttle craft was granted. Yates, Fisher, and LT Washington representing ORION'S crew went down to the science ministry in the City of Vermors. The shuttle touched down at the transportation hub and they were greeted by Rulshaw, head of the ministry. The four men walked down a brightly lit tunnel and caught a travel pod, which took them to the science ministry administration headquarters. Rulshaw escorted the men to his work sector, where the four began the long and arduous task of developing a strategy that would get the travelers back to earth.

"The people of Flox have informed us of your desire to reach your home planet of Earth. I was told by communiqué you have two ships. Our scanners have only recorded one entering our system," Rulshaw referenced.

Yates replied, "The ORION, our sister ship was destroyed in a battle with the Bedzal fleet, along with most of her crew. We have some of her survivors on board, as well as some of her fighter craft."

Rulshaw showed a slight emotional look of remorse, and continued,

"You have brought with you the size and weight of your space ship? I will need this information to calibrate the exact angle to enter the flux tunnel."

"Yates asked, "Flux tunnel?"

"You would not be able to pronounce our word for it, it is a close translation. In space there are fluctuations in narrow voids of space. These are like tunnels that enable ships or objects to travel great distances in short periods on time. The voids move around, but generally stay in any given area. We have mastered how to calculate when they will appear and where they will go. The rotation of planetary systems and the expansion of the universe are the main variables. We are familiar with you system. We had visited it many thousands of years ago," Rulshaw explained. He pushed some buttons and interstellar graphics appeared on a giant screen that circled the room.

Rulshaw called for one of his collogues and handed him the information provided by Yates. As they waited for the 'map' to get back home to be calculated, Rulshaw was very interested in the voyage of the earthlings, and the four men exchanged details and philosophies of the ongoing trek.

The much anticipated results were soon brought back to Rulshaw and laid on his working counter. He reviewed the charts and handed them to Captain Yates.

"This is amazing, they're printed in perfect English," Yates stated.

"The Flox gave us reference of your language. I, as they find it an easy one. Perhaps one day it may be the one used by all," Rulshaw prophesized.

"Do you have any questions before you embark on your journey home?"

"Yes, I have one," Yates advised and then continued. "When we entered the flux tunnel, our ship, as well as the ORION bounced out of control and this caused a great amount of damage and injury. Is there any way to control this effect?"

"A ship entering the flux must do so on its own accord. You must steer the ship slowly up to its opening at the desired angle, then let the vacuum of the flux pull you in. DO NOT FIGHT IT," Rulshaw explained, then with a smile said, "We in the past have done what you did. Any conscientious ship's captain tends to put his vessel in reverse out of fear. This creates a torrent in the magnetic force field. You were fortunate you were not destroyed."

The new associates bid each other farewell and thanks. Rulshaw wished the CONSTELLATION a safe journey. The shuttle returned to CONSTELLATION and the ship left its orbit, to begin her final leg in the journey home.

The star cruiser was about two days away from where the flux tunnel was calculated to be and, as planned, there was one more duty to be preformed - the marriage of Lieutenant John Marsh and Ensign Barbie King.

As the crew gathered in the ship's chapel, they noticed a festive display. Commander Jagman and LCDR Wang, with a host of others had spent the previous night decorating the room with beautiful floral arrangements and paper streamers.

The chapel was full of crew members, all in dress uniform. Father Delaney, Captain Yates, LCDR Wang and Marsh's college buddy, Steve Williams stood at the head of the chapel.

The bridal march started to play and King was escorted to the altar by Commander Edwards. King was nervous and her rosy red cheeks glowed through her veil. Her long white gown was draped with lace that trailed to the end of the long train. The music ended and Father Delaney started the service.

"Who giveth this woman to this man?" he asked ceremoniously.

"I do." Commander Edwards proudly stated.

"Before I continue with this blessed ceremony, let me take this time to welcome all of you here. Our journey has been long and hard, and as we come to its end, I can't think of a happier note to end it on than the sacred union of this man and this woman in the holy bonds of matrimony. A union TRULY made in the heavens," Delaney exclaimed.

The service continued, the Washington brothers sang two songs 'Something' and 'Here, There, And Everywhere' acappella-style. The ceremony ended and a reception followed in the officer's mess. The ship's cooks prepared a twelve layered cake large enough to serve the entire crew.

With the joyous celebration over, CONSTELLATION got back to business the following day. Yates and Edwards toured the ship to ensure anything loose was battened down, in case things went not as planned. It was the eve of the final hurdle home. Yates ordered the ship to half speed and also ordered everyone to get a good night sleep. He wanted a sharp crew for the event on the next day.

Yates reported to the bridge at 0700 hours. The entire staff was full of anticipation.

"Commander Edwards, what is the status of CONSTELLATION?" Yates asked.

"Captain, CONSTELLATION reports all departments ready, everything is battened down tightly, except for the newly weds who, my God, are still going at it," Edwards replied.

"I see," Yates humorously acknowledged." I thought I felt some vibrations in the ship last night."

LT Williams stepped out from the search center and stated,

"Captain, I have our target dead ahead and have plotted our angle of entry into the ships navigational computer."

"Very well, helm as soon as you start to feel the flux's pull, stop all engines and let it pull us in," Yates ordered.

As anticipated, a black hole soon appeared on the ship's main viewing screen. As the black void grew larger, the stars on the screen started to disappear.

"Captain, I'm seeing an increase in speed and am switching the engines to stop," the helmsman reported.

"Very well. Ralf, this is it, we are finally going home," Yates said.

"Won't Space Command be surprised to hear us on the radio! I hope my wife Kate filed the income taxes on time. Otherwise I'm taking the first ship back out here. I'd rather face the Bedzals than the I.R.S," Edwards joked.

The ship's speed started to increase at a faster rate as she was being pulled into the flux. The only thing appearing on the main viewing screen now was the entryway of the tunnel that would hopefully bring CONSTELLATION home.

As the ship entered the space hole, a loud buzz could be heard outside the vessel and a soft vibration could be felt throughout the star cruiser. The viewing screen was now black with lines from electrical charges going through it, very much like a television set on the fritz. The ride was into its second hour and, unlike before, it was very smooth. At times the buzz got louder, but it only lasted for a short period of time.

"Captain, I'm starting to pick up images on the long range scanners," Lieutenant Williams yelled.

"What are they, can you get a fix yet?" Yates inquired.

"Not yet, no wait. Son of a bitch! It's the Milky Way!" Williams laughingly replied.

"We're home Al, by God we made it!" Edwards exclaimed.

Colonel Fisher, who had been waiting with his men, entered the bridge. He saw the excitement.

"Well, I guess my question has been answered. We've made it back, haven't we?"

"Yes Sam, the ordeal is over. Lieutenant Lister, patch me thorough to the P.A. system," Yates ordered.

"Attention all hands, attention all hands. I'm about to give an order and I wanted you all to hear it. Helm, increase speed to three quarters and plot a course back home, home to earth."

Cheers could be heard throughout the ship. The crew couldn't believe they had made it back. Some were weeping from joy, others were dancing, while others held each other and patted each other on the back.

"Mr. Hall, you have the com. Let me know when we reach Mars or Newark, whichever one comes first. Sam, Ralf, would you join me in my quarters for a minute?" Yates asked.

The three men left the bridge and went to Yates's quarters. There the captain pulled out three glasses and filled them with Jamison's. They lifted their glasses and Yates spoke these words.

"To our fallen friends. To unbreakable friendships. To the USS ORION. To the USS CONSTELLATION!"

The three men downed their drinks and threw their glasses against the wall. They stood looking at each other, not speaking a word. It was hard to hold back the emotional outpour that was coming to its peak.

"Gentlemen, I cannot tell you what a privilege it has been to serve with you. I thank you for your loyalty and friendship. We could not have made it home without your leadership abilities. Thank you," Yates spoke softly with his voice wavering.

"Captain to the bridge, Captain to the bridge," called over the P.A. system.

Yates, Edwards and Fisher returned and they were informed Mars was dead ahead. Yates asked Lister to hook up a radio link to earth.

"Space Command Headquarters, this is USS CONSTELLATION. Captain Alex Yates in command. Do you roger? Over."

There was a short silence then came a reply.

"CONSTELLATION, welcome back. Where have you been? Did ORION find you?"

"Space Command, advise of a secure frequency and we will start to download our logs. We will be passing Mars soon and hope to be home in two more days. Also, contact my wife and see if she needs me to pick up some milk on the way home," Yates finished.

The captain walked up to the observation deck and sat down. He stared out into space, reflecting on what he, his crew and ship had been through. He was quite proud of their accomplishments and quite saddened by the losses of his friends. But most of all he was happy to be going home. His thoughts ran mixed in his mind as he recalled incident after incident. His deep thoughts were interrupted by giggling and the sounds of kissing coming from up in front.

"Mr. and Mrs. Marsh, can't you two wait until you get home?" the captain warmly asked.

The two jumped up and started to speak when the captain shook his head and said, "Carry on." Yates turned and walked away.

CONSTELLATION put into earth's orbit and contacted Space Command and requested permission to land. It was granted, CONSTELLATION was told to land at Space Command Headquarters, the same place she had taken off from. Yates gave the order and the star cruiser gently entered the earth's atmosphere and headed towards her final destination.

The massive ship touched down with a perfect landing and taxied to where the hangers once stood that she was built in. Yates and Edwards walked down to the hanger deck where they found the officers of his ship and several officers from ORION standing in formation. As Yates and Edwards entered, they were greeted with cheers and applause. Handshakes were exchanged, and Yates ordered the hanger bay doors to be opened.

As the doors slid open, a navy band stood outside playing 'Anchors Away'. The ramp slid down from the ship and the officers stepped out. They were greeted by a cheering crowd. Admiral Trout was the first to walk up the ramp to greet the returning ship, and he was yelling.

"Yates, were the hell have you been? Do you know the amount of overtime I'm going to have to pay out for the last year and a half? Welcome back, son."

The admiral gave a warm welcoming hug to the captain.

"Al, Ralf. Your wives are being brought aboard on the other side. We have your ship's log being processed. There will be a short meeting today for an abridged version of your trip. After that you and your crew have six weeks off. Matter of fact, after you dismiss your crew, they can leave. We have a packet for them to read. They just can't discuss the mission with anyone until the official releases are put out," Trout stated.

Yates reached over to a phone and plugged into the ship's. P.A.

system and said.

"Attention all hands, as soon as you pack up you have six weeks of leave coming to you. As you are processed out you will be given a packet of what you can and cannot talk about pertaining to the mission. I want to thank all of you for your hard devoted work. It was the team spirit of CONSTELLATION that pulled us through. Thank you all for your efforts. I am proud to have served with all of you. The crews of CONSTELLATION and ORION are the first people of earth to have traveled into deep space. We have done battle with alien races. We have made friends with peoples of other worlds. We have shown all of whom we have met just what the people of earth are made of. They have found we are an honorable and determined people and will not be forced to abandon our morals. There has been a wreath positioned in the hanger bay, in remembrance for those crew members of both ships who didn't make it back, please pay honor as you pass by it. One other thing. CONSTELLATION and ORION is hereby ordered to stand down. DISMISSED!"

The officers stood in the hanger deck and shook each one of the crew's hands as they left. The crew at times let emotions out as they departed CONSTELLATION and said their goodbyes. Some three hours later, Yates and Edwards walked through the empty ship to the officer's mess to greet their waiting wives.

The two veteran space travelers made their way to the officer's mess and entered. They saw the two wives standing on the far side of the hall clutching cups of coffee. Yates and Edwards paused for a moment. The realization that they had finally made it home had just struck them. Now the loneliness of command and the mission started to fade as tears started to flow down their cheeks with a quickened pace the two men went towards their ladies. As soon as Mary and Kate saw them, they ran up to them and jumped into their arms and cried as they hugged and kissed. The long awaited reunion had finally come to pass.

There was a silence in the room as the couples embraced each other. The emotion was so intense no one could talk. Both Yates and Edwards tried several times to clear their throats, finally the senior ship mates were able to speak Yates and Edwards turned to face each and both said simultaneously.

"Whoever leaves last, turn out the lights."

*THE*

*JOURNEY'S*

*WILL*

*CONTINUE !*

# GLOSSARY OF ABBREVIATIONS

| | |
|---|---|
| A.S.C. | ALIEN SPACE CRAFT |
| A.S.C.-1 | ALIEN SPACE CRAFT FIGHTER |
| C.A.P. | COMBAT AIR PATROL |
| CAPT. | CAPTAIN |
| CD | COMPACT DISC |
| CDR. | COMMANDER |
| COL. | COLONEL |
| ENS. | ENSIGN |
| F-56-A | GOLDEN HAWK FIGHTER |
| L.Z. | LANDING ZONE |
| LCDR. | LIEUTENANT COMMANDER |
| LT. | LIEUTENANT |
| LTJG. | LIEUTENANT JUNIOR GRADE |
| M.R.E. | MEAL READY to EAT |
| N.A.S.A | NATIONAL ARONAUTICS and SPACE ADMINISTRATION |
| OPS | OPERATIONS |
| R.P.G. | ROCKET PROPELLED GRENADE |
| S.C. | STAR CRUISER |

| | |
|---|---|
| SGT. | SERGEANT |
| TS-1 | TRANSPORT |
| U.F.O. | UNIDENTIFIED FLYING OBJECT |
| X.O. | EXECUTIVE OFFICER |

www.ingramcontent.com/pod-product-compliance
Ingram Content Group UK Ltd.
Pitfield, Milton Keynes, MK11 3LW, UK
UKHW020133250726
13967UKWH00002B/620